WHAT HAVE I DONE?

BY ELLEN BURMEISTER

PublishAmerica
Baltimore

First printing

ISBN: 1-4137-0739-4

PUBLISHED BY PUBLISHAMERICA, LLLP

www.publishamerica.com

Baltimore

Printed in the United States of America

This book is dedicated to my family and friends who helped in various ways with comments, suggestions, and encouragement. I especially want to thank Rita and Angela Giocomelli for their contributions and my daughter Mary Ellen for all of her help.

CHAPTER 1

It was the fall of 1946. I was sitting in a little cabin in Phoenicia, New York. I was depressed and desperately lonely. I wanted to reach out to my wife, who thought I was dead. I was trying to compose a letter and put my thoughts on paper, but as I sat there on a Sunday afternoon, my thoughts drifted back to the beginning of how all of this started and how I got here. It all started with the war. It started out as just another Sunday afternoon, but my mind grew weary as I contemplated the past.

* * *

Mama and Papa, Carlo and Angela Roman, came to America from Italy in 1927. My brother and I were born in Italy. I was born in 1923; my parents named me Joseph Carlo. My bother was born in 1925 and named Anthony Nicolas. The twins, Camille Angela and Gina Rose, were born here in America in 1930. We came to America on a ship and settled in Hoboken, New Jersey. Papa opened a small butcher shop on the corner and called it Roman's Meat Market. Across the street from the shop was Public Grammar School No. 6. I had graduated high school and worked with my Papa in the butcher shop.

Papa was a short man, but he was robust. His hair was slightly gray, and he had a full face with hazel eyes and a hooked nose. He had a round belly and was very jovial. The nicest thing about him was his smile. He wasn't handsome, but he was good looking in a wholesome kind of way. He may have been small in stature, but he stood tall in his convictions. Papa was a strong, calm man who was able to keep his composure in most situations. Papa's calm, friendly manner made him a great businessman. When people complained about the meat, he would always smile, pause, and say, "Well, I didn't raise the cow; I only sell the meat. I am sorry. Please give us another try." No matter how angry people were when they came in, they usually would leave the market smiling. Papa had such a nice way of treating people.

We rented a small apartment on Eleventh Street. Mama and Papa would have liked to live downtown where Papa's brothers lived. Everyone called it Little Italy because all of the Italians settled down there. There were Italian bakeries, fish markets, and grocery stores. Of course, everyone spoke Italian. Papa could only find a store and apartment to rent on Eleventh Street, so that's where we settled. I think Mama was happier with our apartment because we had our own little water closet with a toilet and sink. The toilet had a tank on top. When you pulled the chain, it flushed. It also had a small window. There was another small room with a bathtub, a wash tub, and a window that led out to the fire escape. Our relatives who lived downtown were not as lucky as we were to have a private water closet in their apartment. They had toilets in the hall. There was one on each floor for two apartments. They took a bath in a wash tub once a week in their kitchen. Mama used to say that the halls smelled in the houses downtown.

When entering the apartment, we would enter into the kitchen. The bathroom was behind the kitchen in one direction, and the bedrooms and parlor were in the other direction. We had four railroad rooms and copper faucets in the kitchen sink that Mama was always shining. There was one window in the kitchen and a wooden table and chairs. Papa made a small replica of our kitchen set from wooden cigar boxes, stained it, and let the girls play with it. The kitchen had wainscoting on the bottom half of the walls and very large cupboards for the dishes. Once we had a little earthquake, and some of our dishes fell and broke. It was a little bit scary to watch the dishes rattle through the glass doors in the cupboards and then fall on to the floor.

We also had an ice box in the kitchen. Mama used to forget to empty the pan under the melting ice, and the water would run downstairs to the apartment under us. Kate and her mother, Bertha Brown, lived below us. Bertha would fuss a little about the mess from the water, and then she would get over it. In some apartments, you could hear people yelling all the way down the street when the water ran down to the next floor. Everyone hated to clean up that mess! In addition to the icebox, we had the luxury of a gas stove and steam heat. A lot of apartments didn't have heat, they had coal stoves.

Next to the kitchen was a bedroom that my sisters slept in. It had a double bed and a chest of drawers. It also had a big closet right across the wall with two drawers on the bottom for shoes and a shelf on top for storage. Mama and Papa's bedroom was next to my sisters' room, and they had a full-size bed, dresser, and chest. They also had the same kind of closet as the girls. Neither bedroom had windows. The last room was the parlor, which faced the street. It had a blue area rug with a small print, a studio couch, chest, one chair, and lace curtains on the two windows that Mama stretched on a big wooden stretcher. There was no closet in the parlor, so my brother and I had to hang our clothes on a clothes tree.

Every evening after supper the dumbwaiter would come down from the top floor. The superintendent, Mrs. Ahrens, would call for garbage. Everyone was supposed to place their bag in the dumbwaiter in such a way that it did not fall over, but no matter how much we tried the bags always seemed to topple over. The spilled garbage made the dumbwaiters smell, and when we opened the door to the dumbwaiter in the kitchen, the garbage aroma filled the whole room. This awful smell always seemed to arrive at the dinner hour. Mrs. Ahrens was constantly hollering up the shaft about spills. The garbage cans were stored in the basement, so the basement also smelled.

Each person who lived in our building had a little wood shed in the basement to store things in, but we did not like to go into the basement. We hoped and prayed that Mama would not send us downstairs to get anything for her. It was dark and smelly down there, and it was a place that would make your imagination run wild with fear.

On steamy summer days Mama would let the girls sit on the fire escape and blow bubbles. She told the girls never to stand up on the fire escape because they could fall over the side. One hot summer day, Mrs. Stevens' little black Scotty dog actually jumped over the rail of the fire escape and landed down in the yard. Mrs. Stevens and her two boys ran down the apartment stairs to rescue the dog from the fate we all feared. However, the little dog lay very still and did not move. We held our breath as Mrs. Stevens slowly turned the dog over only to find that it was dead. She began to rub her eyes and sob softly. Her two sons, Billy and Bobby, tried hard to console her. I wanted to feel sorry for them, but I just couldn't find the feelings within my heart. They always bullied Tony and me and called us wops or guineas. Mama told us to ignore their cruel names, but it hurt us. I think this accident also convinced the girls never to stand up on the fire escape again.

Meal times were the happiest times of the day. We always ate dinner at 6 o'clock. Mama was such a good cook. Sunday and Wednesday were pasta days. On Sunday we would sit around the table for hours talking. Sometimes Papa's brothers, their wives, and children would come to visit and have pasta with us. Everyone enjoyed waking up to the aroma of tomato sauce cooking on Sunday morning. Mama put a little piece of pork in the sauce to add to the flavor and mouth-watering smell. After Mama started cooking, we would all go to Mass. When we came back from church, Mama would make homemade bread, and sometimes she would make Italian pastry (when we had the money for it). Mama would get the supplies for her great meals on Eighth Street at the dairy. She would bring her little milk pail to buy milk, butter, cheese, and duck eggs.

DECEMBER 7, 1941, HOBOKEN, NEW JERSEY

It was Sunday afternoon, and we were listening to a football game. The announcer interrupted the game to give a bulletin. He said that the Japanese had just bombed Pearl Harbor. America was on alert. Our ships had been bombed and many of our service men had been killed. Wow! How would this change our lives? We had been through so much—the crash in 1929 and the depression that left us hanging on by a thread financially. We were barely scraping by, and we found ourselves asking the question, "Now what?" All kinds of rumors were circulating. Some people were saying that they saw submarines out on Long Island. No one knew what to believe or what the truth was. One thing was for sure—everyone was apprehensive. Pretty soon we would be issued coupons, and food would be rationed. Luxurious, scrumptious meals would be a memory of the "good old days."

I will never forget the uncertainty in the eyes of the children when they returned to school the day after the bombing of Pearl Harbor. Soon after the children arrived at school, Papa and I saw all of the children come running out of the school building. We could see all the excitement through the large windows of the butcher shop. I went outside and asked little Betty O'Brian why everyone was running from the building. She said, "Our teacher told us to run home and not to talk to anyone. I couldn't even put my leggings on. We have to go home, pull down the shades, and stay in the house. We could get bombed. I've got to go!" She quickly turned and ran away in a panic. I went back inside and told Papa about all of the excitement as we watched the children running out of the building in different directions. In spite of this frightening news, we decided to keep the market open until the middle of the afternoon. However, we did not have many customers. Everyone seemed very upset and apprehensive.

After we closed the butcher shop, we went home to listen to the radio to get the recent updates on the bombing. At approximately five o'clock, we had an air raid. We were instructed to shut off all the lights, and we were asked to not even light a cigarette. That wasn't a problem for us since Mama and Papa didn't smoke, but many people in our community did. We had to pull down the shades, close the curtains, and stay in doors. Civil defense workers wore white helmets and worked diligently to patrol the streets. All activities were canceled, and everyone sat silently in the dark waiting for the worst to happen. If the patrol workers saw one little light on, they would come running into the building and knock at the door with a nightstick demanding that all lights be turned off. Sometimes, they banged on the door so hard we thought the glass panels on the door would break. I remember one time we sat in the dark for a long time looking at one another not saying a word, and then Papa broke the silence and said in a soft, somber voice, "Yes, I think life will change. How can it stay the same?" Those words rang in my ears for many months to come.

Sometimes, women would run downstairs to the grocery store when their children were napping, and the siren signaling an air raid would sound. Mothers would get hysterical and cry because they thought they would be away from their children for just a few minutes. However, when the alarm sounded, the rule was no one was allowed on the street during an air raid. There were no exceptions.

Chapter 2

Living in Hoboken was like having a large family; everyone knew each other. The city was called "the mile square city." We lived in a row house with two families on each floor. Mrs. Ahrens, the superintendent, lived on the first floor on the right side with Kate and her mom on the left. We lived on the second floor, with Mrs. Handon living to the right of us. She was kind enough to let us kids come into her apartment to type on her typewriter and bang on her piano. Dropsy Litewater, an American Indian, lived upstairs on the third floor right over us. He had a refrigerator, so we didn't have to worry about his water pan overflowing down into our apartment. Mama and Papa's best friends, Kitty and Danny DeSantis, lived on the third floor in the apartment to the right of Dropsy Litewater. Kitty and Danny had three children—two girls and a boy. Danny was a bright light in dark times. He was always laughing and playing jokes. He was a barber by trade, but he also tap danced and entertained. He was so full of life and very talkative. Danny was very Italian- looking with black hair, olive skin, brown eyes, a big, round face, large dimples on his cheeks, and beautiful white teeth. He was quite tall. Well, he seemed to be taller than Papa. His wife was sweet and demure. She was slightly introverted, so they made a good pair. She was just the opposite of him. She had blonde hair, blue eyes, and a long face. Kitty rarely smiled, and she had a very calm nature. Danny was definitely the magnanimous person in the marriage.

Danny liked to visit with Papa often. They would laugh and tell stories to each other for hours. One evening when they were exchanging jokes, Danny asked, "Carlo, where's Angela? I would love a big plate of her spaghetti tonight!"

"No spaghetti tonight," Papa answered. "Angela is trying to relax, and she is taking a bath. All this talk about war has made everyone very anxious."

"I think we should try to cheer Angela up," Danny said with a big smile as he pulled a chair over to the bathroom door. "Shhh," Danny whispered with mischief in his eyes. Danny began pushing out the small window over the door to the bathroom. All of a sudden, Mama looked up at the window and let out a hysterical scream. Danny just smiled and said, "Hi, Angela, how are you?" Mama started screaming loudly. I am surprised the police did not come. Mama had large breasts and tried to cover them with her face cloth, but the more she tried, the less she was successful. Papa was very straight laced and would not ordinarily think something like that was funny, but only Danny could get away with mischief like that. Papa chuckled briefly and told him not to do that again.

"Danny, you know that Angela will probably not speak to me for a week."

"Ah, the quiet will be nice for a change," he laughed as he slapped Papa on the back.

As the months went by, we found that we had less to laugh about. Life was starting to change drastically. Everyone needed coupons to buy butter, sugar, and meat. Sometimes we substituted the butter with a clear plastic bag with shortening that had an orange button in the middle of it. Mama would pinch the button, then knead the plastic bag until the orange coloring was mixed in to make it look like butter. Every once in a while the bag would break, and Mama was left with a mess. Then we didn't have the butter *or* shortening. Women fought in the Safeway grocery store over soap powder, and sometimes they would pull on the boxes so hard that all the soap powder would spill on to the floor.

A lot of the staples had to go overseas to the soldiers. It was hard to get coffee, so sometimes we used Postum in its place. Nylon stockings became extremely hard to get, because the nylon was used to make parachutes. Most of the girls wore leg make-up to cover their legs. Rationing was generally accepted as the civilian contribution to the men in combat. Each of us carefully planned how to spend the stamps wisely.

We had enough food to eat because Papa had the butcher shop, but sometimes Mama would make soup because Papa was a little low on meat at the market. Papa always gave a little extra to pregnant women and families that had a lot of children. We didn't have much, but Papa had a big heart and wanted to make sure no kids went hungry. It was Papa's custom to give kids a slice of bologna when they came into the store. Sometimes the meat Papa would bring home was tough, and Mama would tell us to chew the juice out of the meat, and then spit it out.

Watching the tragedy of war unfold made us think of the Depression years when things were very difficult for us. Either we couldn't get meat, or when we did get meat, it didn't taste very good. During the worst years of the depression, Papa only sold to professional people such as bankers, teachers, etc. (anyone who had a steady income). There were so many people out of work. I suppose if there was anything positive about this situation, it was that all of us were in the "same boat," so we had to work together to survive. Very few people had any money. Many times Papa gave a little meat to families he knew had no food; and Mama would make bean, chicken, beef, or mutton soup. Mutton didn't seem difficult to get, but it was so tough. There were butchers who sold horse meat, but many people did not want to buy that type of meat. We all hoped things would not get as desperate as they did during the Depression years.

In addition to all of our problems, it felt like this was the hottest summer we'd ever experienced. Lots of flies were sticking to the flypaper, and sawdust was becoming hard to get, so we had to leave it on the floor of the butcher shop for long periods of time. Right outside of the shop in the middle of the street was a cement island separating the street into two sides. It had a few trees on it, which were cut down for the scrap drive. We were all asked to participate in the scrap drive as part of our civic duty. Everyone brought rubber tires, newspapers, all types of metal, foil, and anything that could be used for the scrap drive. We all felt a real sense of pride in helping our country. We became so conscious of saving things for the scrap drives that I even started saving the foil from my gum and making a ball out of it. As our neighbors gathered to visit with each other in the evenings, I would ask everyone if they had any foil from their gum, and I would add it to my foil ball. Eventually they stopped wrapping the gum in foil, but we still saved everything. We had to help the war effort. The scrap drives lasted a couple of weeks, and right before they came to pick up everything, the newspaper sent a photographer to take a picture for the local paper. I was in the picture and felt really good about helping my country. There was a sense of pride and community.

A tall man dressed as Uncle Sam in a red, white, and blue costume with a high hat and white beard visited the schools. He encouraged the children to buy war stamps. The stamps were ten cents apiece and were placed in a little book. When people reached $18.75 worth of stamps, the book could be taken to the to the bank, and the bank would mail them a $25 war bond. Most of the children participated in this effort as their part in helping the war.

Mama was also very conservative and did her part to support our country. She would save little pieces of soap, place them in a jar, let them melt, and then use the pieces to wash clothes on her scrub board. We didn't have the luxury of a washing machine. Papa's brother's wife, Jeanne, had a washing machine. Jeanne had four children and did not let them change their clothes too often. Her washing machine had a round tub on four legs with a ringer made of two rollers on top. She placed their clothes in the machine and let it run for a while, rinsed them in the wash tub, and then put them in the wringer to squeeze out the water. The wringer was at the top of the machine. She faced the machine towards the wash tub so the water would go into the wash tub from the wringer. I can remember a few times she caught her fingers in the wringer. She usually hung out three loads of wash on the line and had to wait until each one dried before the next one could go out.

She did a week's worth of laundry on Saturday because she worked at Yardley's soap factory in Union City during the week. If it rained, she washed on Sunday, which she didn't like to do because people frowned on hanging out wash on the wash line on Sundays. Good Italian Catholics rested on the Lord's day and did not engage in any type of work activity. Mama washed a little each day except on Sunday, so I never saw a lot of laundry around our house. We didn't have to buy soap because Aunt Jeanne could get a bag of scratched soap at Yardley's soap factory for a nominal fee. When we were little, she would bring us animals made out of soap. I particularly remember a little white lamb. Mama asked us to leave the soap animals on our dresser for show until they got dirty, and then we could use them.

It wasn't long before mothers hung little square flags in their windows to support their sons who were serving our country. When one of their sons was killed in the war, a gold star would be placed on the flag. Some mothers had several stars on their flag. I wondered when I would be called to serve my country and if my mother would ever place a star on her flag. I loved my country and wanted to serve in any way I could. One of the proudest days of my life was when my parents and I became American citizens when I was twelve.

I enjoyed the summer because everyone would sit outside on the stoop in the evening and converse. Some people just opened their windows, put a pillow on the sill, and leaned out of the windows for some fresh air. There was a warm, neighborly feeling among us, and there was a deep sense of camaraderie in our community. Of course, everyone constantly talked about the war and news of recent deaths caused by the fighting. When we went to the movies, the newsreel was shown before the movie. Some mothers would recognize their sons being killed or wounded on the screen. They would yell in a shrill, hysterical voice and sob uncontrollably as they screamed, "That's my son, that's my son!" Some very distraught women even fainted. The ushers would rush forward to comfort them, and everyone was most sympathetic. There were times when I would get a funny feeling in the pit of my stomach as I watched our men being slaughtered, and I wondered when it would be my turn.

Evenings were time for thinking and dreaming. I often let my thoughts drift back to happy times in my childhood years. I enjoyed letting my thoughts drift to the little carousel that pulled up to Eleventh Street. I would see it through the large glass window at the butcher shop. Sometimes it was a truck, and other times it was pulled by a horse from Marshall's Stables located downtown. For two cents, the little children could have a ride. My sisters still enjoyed riding the horses on the carousel. I would watch them and think how nice it would be to be a child with no worries about war. All children had to think about were their friends, playtime, and candy. Mama kept pennies in a jar, and my sisters used to run off to the candy store and buy two Horton's chocolate bars for three cents, but now chocolate was becoming scarce.

Before we knew it, summer was coming to an end, and our nights on the stoop would just be a pleasant memory. Fall quickly took its place. On September 29, 1942, I received a telegram telling me I was drafted. I had two weeks to report to Fort Dix, New Jersey. I was very concerned about Papa running the butcher shop alone, but he reassured me that my bother, Tony, would help him. Tony wasn't as serious as I was about work, but he would have to help Papa after school and on Saturdays. It was time for him to grow up now. My family gave me all of the respect that the first-born son deserves. They were proud of me for wanting to serve my country, and I was proud to be an American. I wasn't too happy about leaving my family to go to war, but I knew it was the right thing to do. Mama always taught us to do the right thing. The girls looked up to me as their big brother. I assured Camille and Gina I would be returning soon and told them to help Mama around the house. That night Tony and I had a hard time falling asleep. We talked about many things, and I teased him about having the room all to himself.

Tony and I would constantly fight about where to put our things. I was the neat one, and he was the one who threw his stuff all around the room. Tony and I looked very much alike. Everyone knew that Mama had twins, but many people thought that Tony and I were the twins because we looked so much alike. Unlike our parents, we were tall and thin with brown hair, greenish hazel eyes, and oblong faces. We had Papa's nose, but all the girls that came into the shop thought we were cute because we had big dimples on our chins. The twins were not identical. They looked like sisters, but definitely not twins. They had dark blond hair and light hazel eyes. They were short like Mama and Papa. They took after Mama's family and had round faces with little pug noses and very full lips. They became more beautiful as the years passed.

I knew it would be difficult for Tony and I to say goodbye. It seems like families of immigrants were especially close. We had no one else. Papa had two brothers who came to America, Mario and Giuseppe, but all of Mama's family stayed in Italy. Our family was very important to us, and our whole life revolved around our family times. I did not look forward to all of the changes that were about to take place in our lives.

CHAPTER 3

I had the hardest time telling my childhood sweetheart, Maria, that I had been drafted. We had been sweethearts since I was in the sixth grade. I can't remember how many papers I had confiscated by Miss James, my sixth grade teacher, for writing Maria's name over and over on my paper instead of doing my lessons. When things would get boring in school, I would write Maria Celli all over my papers. Her name transported me to another world.

I waited until after church on Sunday to tell Maria the news. Mama invited Maria over for pasta. I had already told Mama and Papa that my draft papers came, and they were not surprised. They expected it. Dinner was not ready when we came in, and everyone was gathered together in the kitchen, so I asked Maria to come into the parlor with me. We had been together too long for her not to notice that something was amiss. She looked at me very soberly and asked, "Joe, is something wrong?" I answered by asking her to sit down on the studio couch. I then proceeded to tell her that I was drafted. She looked stunned. I suppose that in

ELLEN BURMEISTER

the back of her mind she knew I would be drafted. Perhaps she thought that by not facing the truth it would somehow be forgotten, or disappear. She said nothing; dead silence filled the room. She stared out the window with a glaze on her face as if she was thinking, "This can't be happening." She tried to compose herself. However, when she began to open her mouth to speak, no words would come out. All she could do was cry. Teardrops ran down her face until they dropped into her lap staining her navy blue dress. I felt like crying too, but I was a man, and men are not supposed to cry. There was no conversation; I just held her tightly. After some time, I looked into her beautiful face and told her I would write everyday. She said that she would, too. We vowed to love each other forever and agreed that we would get married when I got out of the service. We had talked about being married since grammar school, and we knew that there was no one else for us. We only wanted each other. Maria's face looked angelic to me. She had long black hair, brown eyes, and a round face. By now, her eyes were swollen, and her nose was running, but she still looked beautiful to me. I could never forget that face. Her hands were delicate and nice to hold. I couldn't imagine how it would feel to be separated from her. I was 20 years old and out of school for a little over a year. Maria was 18 and had graduated in June. She worked in Fisher-Beers Five and Dime Store on Washington Street. Maria said she would save as much money as she could. She made forty cents an hour.

I was glad to hear Mama's voice call, "Dinner is ready. Everyone come to the table." My family already knew about the draft notice, so they had time to compose themselves, and they tried hard to comfort Maria. The atmosphere was a little tense, so papa tried to be playful and cheerful. When mama walked by the table, he pulled her apron string to get her attention. He used to do that when he wanted to get Mama a little flustered. She would pretend to get angry, but I think she liked the attention. Mama was pleasingly plump, very round, and short in height. Papa used to say she was his little ripe tomato. Her cheeks were chubby and usually flushed, but she had very smooth skin. She had brown hair with a little gray on the sides, and she had eyes that danced when she spoke. She had a few laugh lines around her eyes, and she wore her hair in a bun. She usually dressed in black or navy to hide her round shape.

After dinner, Maria and I went to the park. The family understood that we needed to be alone, so none of the kids asked if they could come along. Columbus Park was on Ninth and Clinton Streets and was one of our favorite places. It had a fishpond with goldfish in it, and there was a cement carving of King Neptune on the wall above it. He had long hair, and his mouth was open with water coming through his mouth into the pond. Everyone in the community used the park. The old retired men sat in the park every day talking, children played in the playground, and there was a baseball field in the back. Lovers like us sat on the benches that surrounded the pond and watched the fish. I knew Maria and I would fondly remember this beautiful fall day with the leaves glistening in the sun. The leaves were a vivid gold, orange, and burgundy. We tried to figure out which leaves had the prettiest colors. There were no trees on Eleventh Street. They had all been cut down. So, going to the park was like being in the country. Sitting on the bench holding hands, looking at the water, and watching the fish swim was so romantic and relaxing.

Why couldn't life just remain like this? Why did everything have to change? Why did Maria and I have to be separated? This separation felt like it would last for a lifetime.

We stayed in the park until dusk, and then I walked Maria home. She only lived around the corner from me, so it was not a long walk. However, tonight I wished she lived several miles away, so we could enjoy walking arm in arm together. As we walked, I wondered if her parents would be home and have the stoop light on. I stopped at the corner, and we embraced for several minutes. "Maria, I love you, and I wish I didn't have to go," I whispered in her ear. She kissed me passionately yet gently and whispered, "I love you, too." Her eyes begin to fill up with tears, and I could feel my heart pounding and tears began to flood my soul. I turned away and began to walk briskly toward Maria's house. We held hands so tightly that I thought I would break Maria's delicate hand.

"Goodnight, Maria, I'll be thinking of you," I said as I caught Maria's dad out of the corner of my eye looking out the window.

"I better go!" she said and kissed me on the cheek. As I walked away, I could still taste one of her salty tears on my lips.

The next two weeks flew by quickly. Maria and I continued to see each other as much as we could. I still worked in the butcher shop with Papa. Everyone who came into the store would hear Papa say, "My son is going into the service, so say your goodbye now because in two weeks you will not be seeing him in the store." The goodbyes seemed to go on forever and were very draining. Men were slapping me on the back and shaking hands, and women pulled out their handkerchiefs to wipe a few tears. I left home in the middle of October. It was such a heart wrenching experience leaving my beloved family. I couldn't look at Mama as we all stood in the kitchen. She had a deep sadness in her eyes, which spoke the fear of death to my heart. Papa was trying to stay strong, but when he put his hand on my shoulder, I could feel his hand trembling. Tony tried to act like a man holding back his tears and smiling, but every time he squinted his eyes, little drops of water rolled down his cheeks. The twins, Camille and Gina, just threw themselves on me and wept uncontrollably. I could see Mama out of the corner of my eye crying silently into her handkerchief. I was thankful that Maria was not here and that we had said our goodbyes the night before.

I had to keep a stiff upper lip for my family. I wanted to cry along with them, but I was a man now. I did not feel like a man, and I was forcing feelings that were not there. I didn't want to leave my family and my precious Maria, but it was time to go. Papa walked me to the bus terminal on 14th Street. I wasn't taking too much with me, so together we carried my meager belongings. We didn't say much when we got to the bus station. Papa put his arms around me, kissed both of my cheeks, and said, "My first born son... I am so proud of you. Words cannot express how I feel this day." I boarded the bus and waved to Papa. I watched from the window until he was out of sight. As soon as I could no longer see him, I let out a deep sigh and felt a river of tears flow down my face.

The ride to Fort Dix was uneventful, but sitting on the bus brought back so many memories. I smiled as I thought about my youth, my family, and my first love. The bus was exceptionally quiet, and it appeared that I was not the only one headed for Fort Dix. I noticed that when service men got on the bus that the bus driver would put his hand over the coin collector and not collect any fare from them. I also noticed if a service man got on the bus with a girlfriend, and they needed two seats together, someone would get up and give them a seat. Some of the service men sat in the back of the bus and shared some passionate moments with their girlfriends. Having been brought up very strict, I couldn't imagine myself being on public display like that, but this was wartime, and I suppose anything goes.

As soon as we arrived at Fort Dix, we were assigned barracks. I took the bottom bunk, and my bunkmate, Pete Previte, took the top one. After a brief conversation with Pete, I learned that he was from downtown Hoboken where Papa's brothers lived. We had some interesting stories to swap but definitely not a lot of time. We started our basic training immediately, and it was exhausting. I faulted on my promise to Maria to write everyday. Twice a week was just about all I could handle.

I fell into bed every night feeling muscles I didn't even know existed. My body ached, and my heart ached for my family and Maria. I had never been away from my family before. This was a first for me. The sergeant was tough on us, and I quickly got the feeling that we better take him seriously and do as we were told, or else. He didn't mince words, and he set everyone straight right off the bat. The training was vigorous, and one day ran into the next. Sometimes it seemed like I was there so long, and other times the days went by quickly. We always had something to do, and we were always tired. I really was not used to all this exercise having worked in the butcher shop. I did play some sports when I went to Demarest High School, but since I graduated, I didn't exercise at all, and it sure did take its toll on me. Nighttime was the loneliest. Some nights I was so overtired that I couldn't fall asleep;

other nights I would put my head on the pillow and conk out immediately.

Then there were the nights when Pete and I were awake at the same time. He would talk about his girlfriend, Pat, and, of course, I told him about Maria. When we were hungry, we talked about all of the great food our Mama's made. We described all our favorite foods in great detail. The food they served here in the mess hall was very different. Maybe that's why they called it a mess hall because a lot of food was all slopped together.

On the nights I could not fall asleep, I would just lie there and think about Maria for hours. I would think about all the plans we made and how this separation was affecting us both. I longed to see her. One night, when I was particularly lonely, I thought about getting married on my furlough, which would be right before Christmas. I felt certain Maria would say yes if I asked her, and then we could be together before I was shipped out. I decided that the next day I would sit down and write to her. I was so excited with the idea that I could not sleep all night. I kept telling myself to calm down and go to sleep. I kept picturing how tired I would be the next day, but talking to myself was futile, and sleep did not come. The next day was difficult, but after supper I began to write my letter. The words seemed to flow from the pen onto the paper. After all, I had all night to think about what I would say.

Dear Maria,

I love you so much that my heart aches when I think about being separated from you. There are even some evenings when I cannot sleep, and I can feel tears stream down my face because

I miss you so much. I know men are not supposed to feel this way. As I was growing up Papa always used to say, "Be a man and be strong." But to tell you the truth, I feel like a lovesick boy. I cannot live without you. I am helplessly and hopelessly in love with you. Will you marry me on my furlough? I want you to be my wife more than anything else. With the uncertainty of the war, who knows what our futures may hold?

I want to come home from this war, find you waiting for me, get a little apartment, and start the family we have always talked about. Please say YES. I will wait anxiously for your reply.

All my Love,
Joe

P.S. Please answer quickly!

The next six days seemed like an eternity, but on the seventh day, my name was called, and there was a letter from Maria. My heart raced rapidly, and my sweaty hands shook as I quickly opened my letter.

My Dearest Joe,

Yes, yes, yes, I will marry you. I love you and want to be your wife. I have been wishing with all my heart that you would ask me to be your wife. It would make my life complete to become joined with yours. I am looking forward to seeing you soon and making all our dreams come true.

All my love now and forever,
Maria

I was able to get a ten-day pass over Christmas, and permission was granted for me to be married. I had a few more weeks to think this over. The more I thought about it, the more I was sure I had made the right decision. After making our wedding plans, the days seemed to fly by quickly. Before I knew it, I was on a bus going home to be married. I knew this would be the best Christmas I would ever celebrate!

CHAPTER 4

I left Fort Dix the morning of December 22nd. Then I went to New York City, changed my bus, and arrived at the 14th Street terminal late in the afternoon. I only had a few blocks to walk home, and it was already dusk. It sure did look like it was going to snow. I hoped it wouldn't. I didn't want any complications on our wedding day. As I walked through the chilly street, I kept picturing Mama in the kitchen. I knew Papa wouldn't be home yet. Tony probably wouldn't be home either. Both he and Papa would come in at the same time after work. I was sure Mama and the twins would be there. I couldn't wait so I began walking quickly. When I came to Number 6 School, I turned left and looked up the block. I counted the houses until I saw 252. I ran up the front steps, opened the door to the vestibule, flung the second door open, and ran up the stairs. I knocked on the door with great urgency. Camille answered and jumped into my arms. Gina jumped on her, and the two of them clung to me as if they had not seen me in years. Mama was washing dishes at the sink. When she heard all of the noise we were making, she turned and ran to me.

We stood there in a great huddle hugging and kissing. One thing about Italian families—we all know how to be affectionate.

After my warm reception, I walked to the back of the apartment to the parlor to put my things down. The Christmas tree caught my eye, and the colored lights with the tiny lampshades that spun around on the tree lights mesmerized me. These lampshades had been part of our Christmas decorations for 12 years. They were made of printed paper. Some of them had boys dressed in band uniforms playing instruments. One of them had the Madonna, child, and a star; another had a horse and carriage being pulled in the snow with a dog running behind. The lampshades were placed on a little paper cone that had a pin in the center. It was placed on the bulb, and the heat of the bulb made the shades twirl like a ballerina. The pine smell of the tree, the shining Christmas ornaments, and the lights were beautiful.

Mama always mixed Lux soap flakes, made a paste, and put it on the branches to look like snow. The soap on the tree looked just like snow! I got a warm feeling looking at the tree and remembering all of our past Christmas holidays. I began laughing to myself as I thought about Mrs. Ahrens yelling up the stairs as Papa took the tree out last Christmas after the holiday was over. Mrs. Ahrens would fuss and yell about the trail of pine needles and dried soap that would fall on the stairs and in the vestibule. Oh well, it certainly was worth all the trouble to have such a beautiful tree even though we knew there would be problems removing it.

Mama had a few gifts under the tree, but I noticed she wrote my name and Maria's name on the tags. I guess Christmas gifts would be addressed to both of us in the future. Mama wrote and said she wouldn't be giving us many gifts because I would be leaving, and we wouldn't be setting up housekeeping right away. They didn't have much to give this year anyway, but it simply did not matter. I felt happy and warm inside to be home with my family, and feelings of great anticipation filled my thoughts about the wedding tomorrow. I didn't see Maria that night, but she sent over a note with her ten-year-old brother, Dominick. It read:

> *Dear Joe,*
> *I love you so much, and I can't wait until tomorrow when we will be one. I would love to see you tonight, but I had to work today, and I have so much to do to get ready for tomorrow. See you tomorrow, my darling, and all the rest of our tomorrows!*
>
> *Love always,*
> *Maria*

Mama had baked some Christmas cookies, and I helped myself to some with a cup of Postum. Even the smells in our apartment made me feel good to be home. Papa and Tony arrived home at six o'clock on the dot, and there were more hugs and kisses. We all sat down to eat, and Papa said grace before the meal. As I lifted my head, all I could think of was how our lives would never be quite the same after tonight. I had a feeling of fear mixed with happy anticipation churning inside of me. My mind drifted for a few minutes, and I started to think about when the war would be over, and I would return to my wife, Maria. I thought about our children and how they would be sitting around the table with all of us sharing in the warmth of our family's love. Our family would just grow bigger, and there would be more happiness to share.

We sat around the table for several hours and enjoyed each other's conversation. It was interrupted by a soft knock on the door. Gina got up from her seat and asked Kitty, our neighbor, to come in and have some Postum and cookies with us. Kitty refused our hospitality but extended an invitation to Papa. "Carlo, Angela will be up until all hours tonight getting ready for the dinner tomorrow. I know you are tired after working all day, and Angela told me that you plan to work a half day tomorrow. Danny and I want you to come upstairs to our apartment and sleep on the couch tonight. I know you like to get to bed early, and a good night's rest is important to you. My children are already sleeping, and it will be nice and quiet."

Mama encouraged him to sleep upstairs in Kitty and Danny's apartment. She got out his pajamas, robe, and slippers, and he hurried up the stairs. Kitty followed behind him, so she could make sure that she got him settled with sheets, a blanket, and a pillow. I went into the parlor and read for while. I was so tired that I fell asleep by 10 o'clock. The next morning we were up early, and you could feel the excitement in our apartment. Papa got dressed upstairs and came down to eat half way through our breakfast. He had just sat down at the table when Danny came running down the stairs knocking on our glass-paneled door with great urgency. Mama answered, and her eyes grew in size as she studied the expression on Danny's face.

"What's wrong, Danny?"

"Carlo and you must come upstairs immediately," Danny said as he breathed heavily. "It's very important that I speak to both of you right away!"

No one invited me to come upstairs, but I figured that anything serious required all of us to go. I motioned to the entire family seated at the table to follow me. We filed one after the other upstairs without saying one word as if we were about to investigate some serious crime. We all piled into the kitchen and Danny said, "Please step into the bathroom." Mama looked at Papa with her eyebrows raised and her fingernails in her mouth.

We all walked behind Danny, and there to our astonishment was a piece of toilet paper with a bowel movement lying on the floor. Danny looked at papa very intensely and said, "What is this? I invite you to sleep in my apartment and use my bathroom, and you don't even deposit in the toilet? Why would you do this to me?"

Mama always got her rash when she got nervous, so her face, neck, and chest were very red. However, Mama's rash was nothing compared to the intense crimson heat that radiated from Papa's face. Papa stuttered out the words, "I am sorry, I am mortified . . . I am disgraced, shocked, and puzzled about how this happened. I don't know . . . maybe it happened in my

sleep . . . perhaps I was sleep walking. We stood there for several minutes in silence. Mama was on the verge of tears. This wasn't something you did when invited to stay at someone's apartment. After faltering words and many excuses, Papa said, "All I can do is offer to clean it up."

"Well, go ahead because I am not going to do it!"

Papa almost died of embarrassment as he bent over to pick it up. Suddenly there was a very funny expression on Papa's face. He began to squeeze this firm form in his hands, and he discovered that it was plaster of Paris. Papa breathed a deep sigh and gave Danny a nasty look. Papa threw the firm surprise in the trash, took Mama by the hand, and departed abruptly. However, you could hear Danny laughing all the way down the hallway.

"When will that man grow up? Some of his jokes just aren't funny, especially on a special day like today!"

Once downstairs at the breakfast table, Mama and Papa had a brief discussion about the situation. They both came to the conclusion that Danny went too far today, and they saw no humor in his antics. After they talked about the situation, we all finished our breakfast in silence. I think that Mama momentarily believed that Papa might have created that accident on the floor because one other time when Papa slept upstairs, he created quite a scene. He got up to use the bathroom in the middle of the night, and instead of going back to sleep on the couch, he got in bed with Kitty and Danny. I suppose it was an innocent mistake since our apartment was arranged exactly like theirs. We could hear Danny yelling all the way down in our apartment.

"What the heck are you doing, Carlo? This ain't your bed!"

Danny went around town telling everyone that Papa had gone to bed with his wife and didn't even have the decency to wait until he wasn't home. Danny just loved to hang around the butcher shop and share this story with the customers. This kind of talk made Mama very angry.

After breakfast, we got ready for the wedding. The service was to be held at Our Lady of Grace Church on Fourth and Willow Street at 2 o'clock. Papa had two acquaintances from the butcher shop who offered us cars for the wedding. One car was a 1941 four-door Buick, and the other car was a two-door Chevrolet sedan. Papa sent the four-door Buick to Maria's house because of the girls' dresses, and the rest of us squeezed into the Chevrolet. When the car arrived at Maria's house, her mom took pictures with a box camera. I am glad her family was able to borrow a camera because our family did not own one. The pictures had to be taken outside where there was plenty of light. It was a little cold, but thank God it was a sunny day.

After they took pictures, they all got into the car. Right around the corner, our family was getting into the car at the same time. We both drove down to Fourth Street and arrived at the church at the same time, about 1:50 p.m.

When we got to the church, Papa's family had already arrived. Aunt Jeanne, Uncle Mario, , and their four children—Iris, Angela, Victoria, and Nunzeo—sat huddled together in the fourth row. Papa's other brother, Guiseppe, Aunt Lena, and their two children, Nicholas and Andrea, sat right behind them. Kitty and Danny were there with Anna, Bobby, Josie, and my twin sisters. Most of Maria's relatives were still in Italy, as were Mama's, so there were just a few cousins from Maria's mother's side of the family. There were also a couple of family friends present. It was a very small wedding, but truthfully I did not care if anyone was there. I only had eyes for Maria.

As Mama walked down the isle in her navy dress with a white collar, cuffs, and a small belt, she held back the tears. Her small pillbox hat with a little veil appeared to shake slightly, but she looked beautiful in her white gloves, navy shoes, and matching pocketbook. Papa had a stoic look on his face as he marched down the isle in his dark gray suit, white shirt, and gray tie with a little design on it. He looked as though he was going off to war.

Tony looked handsome in his navy suit that he borrowed from his best friend. He had a white shirt and a navy tie with a red design on it. He smiled so big that all of his teeth showed as we went into a little waiting room until the girls were ready. The twins showed off their gorgeous burgundy velvet dresses with white lace trim and black Mary Jane shoes.

As soon as the organ music started to play, we came out of the room and walked to the front of the aisle. When I saw Maria in her mother's wedding dress, she took my breath away. She looked regal. Her dress was satin on top with lace over it and lace on the bottom. The skirt came under her knees in the front, and it had a little train in the back. She had a lace veil, and she carried a bouquet of white roses with green fern and a big white satin bow. She gave me a quick wink and a nod of approval when we met at the altar, and I knew she thought I looked handsome in my uniform.

Maria's mother, Isabella, had on a very plain dark green dress with a string of pearls around her neck and matching earrings. Her dad, Johnny, had on a navy suit and tie, and her little brother had brown knickers on with a white shirt, a brown tie, and a brown sweater over it. He looked quite dapper with his cap on his head.

Maria's best friend, Roseanna DeNapoli, borrowed a dress from her friend who was recently in a wedding. It was dark pink velvet on top with a tulle bottom. She carried a bouquet of pink roses with green fern and a big satin pink bow.

As I looked down the aisle, Maria looked radiant. However, her dad, who was standing next to her, was very pale, and sweat was pouring down his face. I guess the stress of giving his little girl away was beginning to get to him.

As soon as everyone was seated, the wedding march began to play, and Maria started walking down the aisle. I noticed her face looked flush, and her hands were shaking. I hoped her father would not faint, and I wondered if she was anxious because her father was so nervous. Nevertheless, Maria held her composure. When she finished coming down the aisle, her dad pushed her veil back, kissed her cheek, and sat next to her mom.

Monsignor A. B. Peterson was officiating at the wedding. He invited Maria and me to step up to the altar to take our vows. Maria and I were unsure of what was ahead of us as we physically and emotionally took that big step. I was sorry we did not have the marriage counseling classes that the church generally offers, but they were waived for us since I was away serving my country.

When we started taking our vows, Maria began crying and totally lost her composure. Monsignor had to ask her several times to stop crying. Towards the end of the ceremony, all she could do was shake her head. She wasn't even able to say the words. We took communion together, and drank from the chalice that was engraved with the Imperial Arms of Emperor Napoleon III. When we finished exchanging our vows, we placed rings on each other's fingers. We purchased the rings at Abelson's because they allowed us to pay them off over a period of time. I wanted Maria to have a nice ring.

As I stood at the altar, I was in awe at how beautiful the inside of this church looked. It was completely redecorated in 1941, and its Gothic design was astounding. I had never stood this close to the altar because we were not allowed to stand inside of the railing. As I stood there, I felt very blessed to be getting married in such a magnificent church. I was told that its dimensions were 200 feet in length and 96 feet in width. Even the organ was one of the nation's most famous ones. It was majestic and unusual in its sound and melodic performance. I could hardly believe that I was getting married to the girl of my dreams, on a beautiful day, in a glorious church filled with so much love and with family and friends.

The next thing I knew Monsignor told me to kiss the bride, and the ceremony was over. I wanted to savor every moment, and now it was time to go. Maria and I walked down the aisle with Tony and Roseanna in back of us followed by our family and friends. After our congratulations, we took some pictures outside of the church with the box camera, and then we returned to our cars. We went back to Mama and Papa's apartment with our relatives and friends to enjoy the fabulous dinner Mama had prepared.

It looked like we had a very small wedding in the church, but when we got back to the apartment, it looked like we were having a large reception. We had wall to wall people in the kitchen. Mama borrowed a few tables from the neighbors, and Papa borrowed some chairs from the funeral home. My parents and Maria's parents got along very well because they came from the same part of Italy known as Poffabro, the Italian Alps, and spoke the same dialect. Everything seemed so perfect, and I hoped our future lives together would be like today.

Papa poured the red wine, and Tony made the toast. He held his glass high as he said, "To Joe and Maria, may this marriage that was made in heaven last through eternity. May you always love each other as much as you do today!"

Papa made the salad with olive oil and vinegar. He also made delicious antipasto. Mama made the lasagna, meatballs, and sausage the day before so all she had to do was heat it up. She also made her fabulous homemade bread. We had a wonderful dinner and a great time visiting together. When we finished eating, Mama made real coffee she had been saving for quite some time for a special occasion like this. After serving the coffee, Mama brought out a three-tier wedding cake with little butter cream roses and a bride and groom on top. It was so pretty, and she labored over it with a heart full of love.

Now it was my turn to shed a tear or two. I could hardly contain myself when we both had our hands on the knife and cut the first piece of cake. Sometimes I wished I wasn't such a sensitive person. Many men feel that it is not manly to show such emotion. However, looking into each other's eyes was heavenly, and it did elicit deep feelings inside of me. I felt like I must be dreaming because this felt too good to be true. I believe this was the happiest day of my life.

After dinner, everyone sat around and talked. The men talked about world affairs as they smoked their cigars, much to Mama's chagrin. She tolerated the heavy scent of cigar smoke because of the occasion, but she definitely did not approve. Maria's parents felt bad that they could not cook the dinner and provide the reception. They had less than we did, and my parents did not want to burden them with all of the preparations for our celebration. Mama did not seem to mind. Besides, she was in her glory when she was in her kitchen. Mr. Celli, Maria's dad, never recovered financially from the depression, and the little work he had was sporadic. He was a mason by trade, and sometimes he did a little tile work on the side.

Papa was preparing to serve a cordial when we heard Mrs. Ahrens yelling in the hallway. She was just the superintendent, but she acted like she was the house police.

"There's a fire. There's a fire. Get out of the building!" Mrs. Ahrens screamed as she ran down the stairs. Mama ran to the door and opened it.

She yelled down the stairs to Mrs. Ahrens. "What's happening?"

"Dropsy Litewater's Christmas tree is on fire!"

Mama panicked and began screaming. "Carlo, get the girls out into the street. Get everyone out into the street!"

It was cold outside, and the kitchen was packed with people. Our guests rushed to Mama and Papa's bedroom to get their coats, and everyone got bottlenecked in the doorway. There was complete pandemonium in our apartment. Mama was a very excitable person, and it did not take much to set her off. She was deathly afraid of fire, and I could almost see her heart beating out of her chest from across the room.

She started screaming, "Hurry, hurry," as the hall filled with smoke. She chased everyone down the stairs and out into the street. It was hard getting everyone out quickly because most of our guests were crammed into the kitchen. Everyone got out except Mama. She ran around the apartment looking for her shawl to cover her head. When she went to go down the stairs, she could not see. Papa ran to the firebox downstairs in the street and pulled the alarm. The smoke completely filled the stairwell, and Mama panicked and went back into the apartment. She sat on a chair in our kitchen, frozen with fear. The smoke made Mama sick to her stomach and made her head spin, but she could not move. She sat on the chair and cried. Then she started to pray, "Dear God, if I die today, please be with my family and watch over them. This was such a beautiful day, and now it is turning into a nightmare. Oh, God, please help us." At that moment, she was overcome by the smoke and slipped to the floor.

Everyone was accounted for outside except Mama, and we became very upset. Tony and I wanted to go back into the building to look for Mama, but you could not see a hand in front of your face. The twins started to wail and became almost crazy with worry, knowing that Mama was inside. Papa just stood there helpless, but he told all of the children that they would not be permitted to go back into the building. Every time we opened the door to go upstairs, big black billows of smoke hit us in the face.

Papa began to tremble as he said, "Oh my God, if anything happens to her, I'll never forgive myself. I shouldn't have come down without her. I thought she was in back of me."

"Papa, don't blame yourself. You know how Mama is. She always has to do one more thing or get one more thing," I said, as I rubbed Papa's back gently.

"This is one more thing that could kill her," Papa said as he wrung his hands. Then he began to console the twins who were shaking with terror.

After sending in the alarm, the firemen arrived in about five minutes. As far as we knew, Mama was the only one left in the building. The fireman told us to stay calm, and they advised us that they would go up the fire escape and try to get her out that way. Two of the fireman headed up to the second floor and climbed in Mama's window.

Several other firemen went upstairs to the third floor to put the fire out. Dropsy's living room was gutted by the fire, but only in the corner by the tree. The couch also caught fire, but the smoke was much worse than the fire. Dropsy had thrown pots of water on the fire, which kept it from spreading throughout the apartment.

The two firemen found Mama in the kitchen, lifted her off the floor, and dragged her down the stairs, which was easier than trying to use the fire escape. She was only half conscious and able to help very little because she was quite limp from weakness and smoke inhalation. When the firemen brought Mama outside, the whole family cheered. They placed her on the stoop and asked if she wanted to go to Saint Mary's Hospital. She did not want to go to the hospital because she felt the fresh air was helping her feel better. She felt sick to her stomach, and her head hurt, but she thought she would be fine. Everyone stayed outside in the cold for over an hour. The firemen wanted to make sure everything was all right before letting us go back into the building.

After we were allowed to return to the building, we opened all of the windows. Mama was really shook up and had to lie down. She kept apologizing to our guests. Aunt Jeanne made another pot of coffee, and Papa offered all of the guests some strong coffee to drink. We didn't want to leave the windows open too long because the cold was coming in, and everyone had to keep their coats on. After about thirty minutes, we closed them a bit and just left them open slightly. Papa commented that he was sorry that he had just had the apartment painted because everything was covered with a brown film and looked like it needed to be painted again. Our parlor got damaged a little from the water, and some of the presents under the tree were water damaged. I suppose it could have been much worse. Mrs. Ahrens came by to tell us that she would try to have the damage repaired in the next couple of weeks. She did not know how long it would take to get someone to come to do the work because of the holiday. Papa said that was fine with him. I think he was thankful that the whole ordeal was over and that mama was safe.

However, Mrs. Ahrens was furious about the Christmas tree fire. We could hear her complaining loudly as she visited each tenant. Sometimes the tenants got angry with Mrs. Ahrens when she went to New York to visit her relatives and didn't get back in time to put the hall lights on. Everyone had to go up the stairs in the dark, and when she returned, she got a "dose of her own medicine."

Dropsy Litewater was very quiet as he walked up the stairs to his apartment. He held his head low and did not make eye contact with anyone, but this was not very different from his regular behavior. He never had much to say, and he usually greeted everyone politely. When I was little, I used to peek out the door as he was coming up the stairs. I expected to see someone with a long braid and hatchet. To my surprise, he never looked like an Indian.

At 8 o'clock, our guests finished up their coffee and cordials. Then they began hugging us and giving us our gifts. Most of the guests gave us cards with cash gifts because we did not know when we would be getting an apartment. It was always Maria's dream that we would spend our first night together in the Waldorf Astoria Hotel, but I needed to see if we could afford it. After everyone gave us our envelope, I went into the water closet and counted the money. When I came out with a smile on my face, she knew we could go. We needed $12.50 for a taxi. It was always Maria's dream that we would spend our first night together in the Waldorf. We changed our clothes, and Maria went around the corner where she lived, dropped off her wedding gown, and picked up her overnight bag for our one-night honeymoon. I went downstairs to the public phone booth and made the hotel reservation. I asked them to place a bouquet of forget-me-nots on the nightstand in our room. I also called for a taxi and told him to come in a half-hour. After all of our goodbyes and good nights, we waited for our taxi to take us to New York City.

The Waldorf wasn't far. We just had to go through the Lincoln Tunnel and up to Park Avenue between Forty-ninth and Fiftieth Street. This was so exciting! We were two kids from Hoboken staying at the Waldorf. We both couldn't believe it was happening. We checked in at the desk and held our heads high like we were the Rockefellers. However, when the bellhop took our meager belongings to our room, it was obvious that we were not wealthy.

When we put the key into the door and entered our room, we could hardly believe our eyes. We had never seen such extravagant luxury. The room was large and cozy.

The walls were painted light blue and there was an ornate blue rug on the floor. The French provincial furniture was elegant, and I felt like the furniture was too nice to use. The bathroom had white tiles on the walls and floors. It had the thickest, most plush towels I had ever seen. Maria's eyes caught sight of the flowers on the nightstand as we investigated our accommodations. I took

Maria's hand and said, "Maria, this is our special flower. Don't ever forget me." Maria looked wide-eyed. She put her arms around my neck and whispered in my ear, "I could never forget you. You are my one and only love." She looked into my eyes and placed her hands on my cheeks. "Joe, you are my life now. I only live for the day of your return." I held her in my arms like my life depended on it.

Maria went into the luxurious bathroom and changed into her nightgown. When she came out in her white negligee, she looked like an angel or a white, fluffy cloud against the light blue background. I got that lump in my throat again and felt a little overwhelmed. Our first night together was better than all of my dreams. It is something I will never forget. We had both saved ourselves for each other, and we had a deep intimacy between us. What we lacked in experience, we made up for in desire. We enjoyed wild passion mixed with gentle tenderness. The uniting of our bodies and souls was the most spiritual experience of my life. I wanted this to last until death do us part.

Our evening together left us euphoric and exhausted. We had been through such an emotional roller coaster. We went through the stress of the wedding, the trauma of the fire, and the jubilation of our honeymoon all in one day! We ate breakfast in our room slowly, trying to make it last as long as possible. After breakfast we got dressed, checked out of the hotel, and took a bus back to Hoboken.

For the next eight days, we honeymooned on the couch in my parents' parlor. Tony had to sleep in the kitchen on an army cot, which he wasn't too happy about, but he was a good sport about it. I was hoping that as Maria and I shared the parlor that no one would walk in on us. The privacy issue was always a big thing in railroad rooms. One time when I was a little boy, I walked into my parents' room early in the morning, and mama was standing there wearing a big peach corset with laces. Papa was stringing the laces and Mama was putting long silver things into the corset called steeles. They were long flat rods that were narrow in size. They slide right into the small pockets of the corset. Garters hung down, and the whole contraption looked odd and very funny. They both seemed very embarrassed and shooed me out quickly. With that in mind, I hoped all of the kids would respect our privacy. I guess we would just have to wait and see who would come storming in with some news of insignificant conversation. Maria and I hoped that the kids were old enough to understand that we needed our privacy.

We arrived home from the Waldorf just in time to celebrate Christmas Eve with my family. Mama was preparing some traditional fish dishes that we would eat in the evening. Maria and I played house and helped Mama prepare the meal. After dinner, we sat around and talked. Mama was feeling much better, but she said she still had a slight headache. At around 10: 30 p.m., we started to get ready for Mass. We had to leave by 11:00 p.m. because late at night the buses only ran every hour. We left at 11 o'clock to attend Midnight Mass at Our Lady of Grace Catholic Church. When we arrived at the church, it was decorated with beautiful flowers; the scent of pine was everywhere. The candles were all lit for High Mass, and the atmosphere was awesome.

When we left the church at 1:30 a.m., we hoped there would be some extra buses running for the holiday, so we wouldn't have to stand out in the cold. Luckily, we didn't have to stand too long out in the frigid air. A bus came along at 2:00 a.m. After we got home, we all went into the parlor to open our gifts. Mama gave Maria and I some dish towels that were slightly wet and smelled of smoke. She also gave us potholders, embroidered pillowcases, and a table cloth. The twins got a new sled and some small things. Tony got a sweater, cap, socks, and a tie. Papa gave mama earrings, and she gave him a pair of cuff links. Maria and I gave Mama and Papa a Statue of Liberty souvenir that we got on our honeymoon. After opening our gifts, we were sleepy so we all retired for the night.

The next morning Mama had a nice breakfast for us, and we went to Maria's parents' apartment for Christmas dinner. Her mom made a turkey, ziti, and a few Italian pastries. It was great that she invited my whole family to dinner, and I knew that we would grow very close throughout the years. Her parents gave us a white chenille bedspread and some kitchen utensils.

We left Maria's parents' apartment about 8:30 p.m. and went back to Mama and Papa's place. We were grateful that we had a place to stay, but everything smelled like smoke. Mama decided not to get the parlor painted until we left because we would have to smell the paint fumes, and there would be too much confusion.

The next couple of days went by quickly. We had a few meals at Maria's parents' apartment, but Mama served us most of our meals. We took long walks each day on Washington Street. We looked in the stores and daydreamed because we had very little money to spend. Mama and Papa gave us some money for a wedding present. Maria's parents couldn't give us much, and my uncles gave what they could. We had to stretch our money and make it last. One time we walked all the way to the end of

Washington Street and went to the Fabian Theater to see a movie. Then we took the bus back home.

We also took walks to the Ninth Street Park, but it was too cold to sit on a bench. The last two weeks had been truly frigid. There was a layer of ice on the pond, and the park was rather desolate. There were no small children playing and no old men sitting on the benches. There was only one little girl walking around the pond, and even though we were quite a distance from her, we were able to recognize her. It was Molly Fredon.

As we stood watching her, she began to walk on the ice. We heard the ice crack and pop a little, and within a minute Molly fell through the ice and disappeared from sight. We ran frantically towards her, and Maria began to call her name, "Molly, Molly, where are you?"

Molly had slipped under the ice! I yelled to Maria, "I can see her under there, but I can't grab her. She is too far from the hole! I can't reach her!" I took a chance and stood very close to where I saw her and jumped on the ice as hard as I could. As I glanced at Maria, she frowned and swallowed hard. Maria was frozen with fright and could not move.

"Be careful," Maria screamed. "You could slide under the ice, too."

I jumped a few more times as hard as I could, and the ice finally broke. I reached down into the icy, cold water and grabbed Molly's arm. I was standing in water that was almost up to my chest. My shoes, socks, pants, and shirt were all wet. "Maria, I need you to help me. Grab hold of Molly."

Maria snapped out of her frozen pose and helped me pull Molly through the hole in the ice. "A few more minutes, and she would have been gone," I said, as I pulled myself out of the hole while holding onto Maria's ice-covered hands. As soon as I jumped out of the hole, I sat Molly up and slapped her on the back a few times. Water splurged out of her mouth, and she began to wail. I carried Molly from the pond and stepped out onto the concrete. Maria kept shouting, "Are you okay? Are you okay?"

"Yes!" I said emphatically. "We're both freezing, so we have got to get to a warm place right away!" I carried Molly across the street to a string of row houses that were sometimes called "The Honeymoon Flats" because so many newly weds tried to get apartments in those buildings. We ran into the vestibule, and Maria pounded on the door of the first apartment we came to and asked the lady that came to the door for a blanket. The lady hurried to get us a blanket as we stood in the vestibule. We wrapped Molly in the blanket, and I ran to Laura's Candy Store on Tenth Street and called an ambulance while Maria stayed with Molly.

When the ambulance came, Maria went with Molly because she was very upset, and I walked home to get out of my wet clothes. Mama was surprised when she opened the door, and I briefly told her what happened. She immediately wanted to feed me and give me Postum. I passed on the food, but I had a quick cup of Postum to help me get warm. After I began to feel my toes again, I stuffed my shoes with newspaper to make them dry. I put on the warmest clothes I had and ran over to Molly's parents' apartment to tell her mom. As soon as I said that she fell through the ice, Molly's mom lost her breath. She began to hyperventilate and just couldn't catch her breath. I sat her down on her kitchen chair and assured her that Molly was going to be okay, but when she heard that Molly was taken in an ambulance, she began to get excited again.

I offered to take the bus with her down to St. Mary's Hospital and told her Maria was with Molly. Finally, she believed me that her little girl was alive, and she put her coat on so that we could walk to the bus stop. All the way to the hospital she kept saying, "I hope Molly is okay."

When we arrived at the hospital, Molly was drinking some soup, and her mother went over to her and cradled her in her arms and just cried. However, Molly was preoccupied thinking about all of the trouble that she would be in when her mother realized she went to the park without permission. Molly knew her mother would be angry that she got her Chinchilla coat all wet once her mother was over the shock of the accident.

Before we left, Molly's mom hugged and kissed us both. She thanked me profusely for saving her little girl. Fortunately, Maria and I were there for her. People in our community took pride in helping each other. Anyone in our neighborhood would have done the same thing for Molly. As we were leaving, Maria put her hand on my shoulder and said, "I hope we have a little girl just like Molly some day."

"Yeah, but I hope she never falls through the ice!"

New Year's Eve we stayed at Mama and Papa's apartment. Maria's family came over, and Kitty and Danny came down for the festivities. We had a little wine for a toast at midnight and brought in the new year with fear of what the future might bring. After midnight Mama put out sandwiches and some potato salad. She also served her famous Christmas cookies, which we all loved and looked forward to all year long. We spent New Year's Day together very quietly with just my family. I hated for this day to end because I dreaded leaving Maria on January 2.

We had the same tearful exit as we had the last time and more instructions from Mama. Everyone was very quiet and pensive. It was all I could do not to break down and cry. The whole family came to the bus this time, and I made a very quick exit. Saying long goodbyes were too emotionally draining. As soon as I saw the bus coming, I gave everyone a quick kiss, shook hands with my brother, hugged Maria, and said, "See you soon, Baby." I hopped on the bus and felt like I was going to my execution. I wondered if everyone felt this way or if my feelings were different from others.

CHAPTER 5

When I got back to Fort Dix, I was told that I would be going to Austria some time in January. No other details were given. I learned quickly that the army doesn't give many details. We were given very strict instructions that when we got to Austria, under no circumstances were we to say in our letters to home where our location was in case the enemy intercepted our letters. Some of the men in our group were saying that they were going to send gum home to their families, and in the gum wrapper they were going to put their location. Many of the guys felt that at least their families would know where they were. The servicemen couldn't receive their mail directly anyway. All mail was sent to a central location with the hope that the mail would be received within several weeks.

I often wondered what it would be like to be in a foreign country. I had a little wanderlust in me but of course never went anywhere. Even though this assignment was dangerous, it had a bit of excitement for me. When we arrived in Austria things were bad. We were replacing other soldiers that had served their time.

There were constant air raids, and our barracks seemed lit all night with the light from bombs dropping. We only stayed four days in the barracks, which were very primitive. Then we headed up to the front lines. The ditches were furrowed out from the previous soldiers. One never knows how he will feel in such a place. It's been said there are no atheists in foxholes, and I believe that.

As the days and weeks dragged by, my hopes began to sink. All of those dreams of having my own apartment with Maria and starting a family began to dissipate. Where was the reality in all of this? I really don't know what I expected, but whatever I had in mind, it wasn't this. I knew why I was there. I wanted to serve my country. But did it have to be like this? Night after night watching men get killed or wounded was wearing on me. I was not prepared for this physically or emotionally. But then I wondered, "Was anyone?" Men don't seem to share their feelings that much, and many of the guys just blew it off. If they had to be there, they had to be there, and that was that.

I remember feeling so patriotic before I came here. I felt it was a privilege to serve my country, and I still felt that way, but deep inside me was a terrible gnawing at my soul. I knew what I should do, and I knew how I felt. I knew my feelings and thoughts weren't right. How does one come to grips with something like this? I was an honest and honorable person, yet my own thinking was scaring me. Some days I felt like I was losing my mind, little by little, like drops of water. I would have a thought and then correct myself. I would say to myself, "Don't think like that." As I became more tired and disillusioned, my thoughts began to focus on what I could do about the situation.

Most of the fellows would talk about their girlfriends, wives, kids and parents. Somehow it all seemed unreal. Trying to separate what was real and what was not real was hard and getting harder all the time. I felt sick all the time, and somehow I could no longer daydream about the future. The only other time I had felt somewhat like this physically was when I was a youngster. Kate, our neighbor who lived downstairs from us, took her nephew, Peter, and me to Coney Island for the day. Mama gave me $.25 to rent an umbrella. Peter and I went over to the stand, paid the $.25 and the attendant said, "Do you want me to put it up for you?" We said, "Oh no, we can do it ourselves." We carried it back to where Kate was sitting and tried to put it up, but we didn't have a shovel so we couldn't place it down far enough in the sand. Consequently, the umbrella kept blowing over and blowing away. Kate finally got exasperated and said, "Forget it, it's going to hit someone." Peter and I sat all day in the sun.

Kate was a nice person but not very patient. She was so beautiful. She looked like the girl in the ads on the billboards for Palisades Amusement Park. She had long black hair, and her face looked like a China doll. She also had a fabulous figure and lots of boyfriends. When we were sitting on the beach, all of the guys were giving her the eye, but she didn't seem very interested. For that matter, she didn't seem very interested in us either. She took us to the beach, and we were kind of on our own. Had she been observant, she would have noticed that we were getting burnt to a crisp from the sun.

Peter was part Italian, but his family was from the South of Italy. He had darker skin than I did. He burned, but not as bad. I was very fair skinned, and when we left the beach, we both started to hurt. We took the train home and started to feel uncomfortable. By the time we reached home, blisters had started to break out, and by evening, I had blisters on my shoulders the size of quarters. It wasn't just the burn, I hurt all over, felt nauseous, had a headache and very bad chills. It's strange the way we can associate feelings. I felt the same way now.

When Mama saw me badly sunburned, she didn't seem too concerned. I think she thought it was a valuable lesson. Her only words were, "If you didn't use the umbrella, you got burned." I tried to explain that we went back to the boy who was renting the umbrellas, and he said, "I can't come now. I have to do it when you pay." Mama wasn't one bit interested in my story, only the lesson learned.

Now I am sitting here thinking, "What am I supposed to be learning here?" I feel terribly torn apart. My parents and I were so grateful that we could come to America. As a youngster, I always felt I would gladly die for my country, but coming face to face with death daily, I was no longer sure of anything. I just wanted to be back on the studio couch in my parents' apartment surrounded by family and friends, or better still, have my own apartment with Maria. This whole scene was so foreign to me. Not only was I in a strange country, but I myself felt strange, like sometimes I wasn't even in my own body. I suppose from time to time I had to detach from the war. I was never so mixed up and confused in my life. I felt like I didn't know myself, and if I did, who was the real me? I couldn't answer that. My thinking did not change overnight, but little by little; on a daily basis I started to entertain thoughts of leaving this place. I knew what would happen to me if I got caught, but I didn't care. The smells were starting to get to me. It reminded me of the smell that blew through Hoboken from the Secaucus pig farms.

I lost track of time after I got shot in the thigh. I had only been on the front lines four months, but it felt more like four years. My wound wasn't deep, but it bled profusely. I was taken to a makeshift hospital, had the wound cleansed and sutured, and was told I would get one pint of blood. I wondered where they would get it.

When the nurse came in with the bottle, she placed it down next to me, and I read the label. It said *Parker Labs, Oakland, NJ Blood Plasma*. The nurse looked at me with raised eyebrows when she saw me reading the label. "That blood plasma came from a blood bank in New Jersey, and it is perfectly safe. We mix it with the sterile water and use it for transfusions," she said in a stern voice.

I knew this powdered blood saved a lot of lives, but I wasn't too happy with the idea of her putting a stranger's blood in my body. Three short days after my transfusion, I was sent back to the front lines. The smell of death and the sight of blood began to make me nauseous. Many thoughts ran through my mind. Most of my thoughts were disconnected. However, I knew I had to get out of this place. I thought of being called traitor, coward, turncoat, and many other names. I knew my family would be disgraced. Papa, who always taught us to be proud of our name, would have to hang his head in shame over his firstborn son. This was the choice for me--either I lost my mind or I left here.

Where would I go? I had to have a plan. I couldn't just get up and leave. I would have to wait until we had a big commotion. Then I could go. It had to be in the evening, and it had to be when everyone was distracted. I myself was terribly distracted. I was cold, hungry, dirty, and homesick. With all of the smells of carnage around me, I could only think of Maria and how she always smelled like flowers. She said she used Cashmere Bouquet talcum powder.

My thoughts vacillated back and forth. Should I, shouldn't I? After awhile, I was doing some involuntary thinking, just scrambled thoughts with not much of a pattern. I asked myself many times if I was having a breakdown. Why couldn't I make up my mind and stick to it? Why was I always changing my mind? Of course, this was not an easy choice. There was so much resting on this decision. In fact, my whole future depended on my resolution. I could get shot on the spot for going AWOL. Sometimes I heard voices in my head that I didn't recognize, and I knew I was losing it. Once I made up my mind, it was a little easier. Several nights after I made my final decision to leave, there was a great deal of bombing, and I knew it was my chance to get away. In the midst of much confusion, I slipped out of the trench and into the woods. I am going to guess that it was about the middle of May. We never knew exactly what day it was. The days were cool when the sun was out, but the nights were very cold. I kept thinking about what we were told in boot camp about not getting too close to a buddy because he may not be there tomorrow. How true that was. Hearing it and seeing it were so different. I felt like I was deserting my buddies that I had been with for the last several months. Obviously, they would think I was dead. This whole thing was getting complicated the more I thought about it. Maybe I should stop thinking about it and just concentrate on staying alive and getting to my destination. I knew the trip would be difficult for many reasons. I also knew I would have to walk a lot.

My leg wasn't 100 percent healed, but I didn't see a big problem with that. The mountains were the biggest challenge. Hoboken is one square mile of flat city. I never saw such mountains in my life. They looked like they touched the sky. I knew if I thought about this too much I wouldn't do it, and there were no guarantees in life. Every opportunity I got, I needled myself. Mama and Papa raised me to do the right thing. What in the world was I doing? I knew better. What was forcing me to do this? Despair, I guess. At this point I couldn't even think of the consequences. My only thought was to get far away from this place.

As I began my escape, I was trying to justify what I was doing but couldn't. "I just have to do this," I said loudly to myself. Whether I stayed or left, it was all a game of choice and luck. I wanted to pray, but how could I ask God to help me with something I knew was very wrong? I walked in the woods along side of the road so as not to be seen. The first night I didn't rest at all. When daylight came, I looked for some type of U.S. transportation. I had to make sure before I stepped out that it was one of ours. Every time I heard a vehicle, I hid until I could identify it. Most of the vehicles weren't going very fast.

I waved down the first jeep that came along and asked for a ride. John Martin was driving that U.S. Army jeep. He was from Kansas City, Missouri. I told him that my entire battalion was wiped out and that I was headed to the Italian Alps to get new orders. I told him I thought there was a temporary Army base there. I am glad he believed me. Most of the groups were young like me and didn't know much about the area. I was fortunate that he believed my story. He took me as far as he was going and let me out. I asked him if he had a candy bar, and he gave me one. I walked again until dark and found a spot in the woods for the night. By this time, I was very tired and cold and tried to sleep but couldn't. I only slept sporadically. I figured if I could sleep, I wouldn't be so hungry. I knew I needed my rest but knowing it and getting it were two different things.

As I lay on the ground, I began to think about the potato chips I longed for as a child. There was a glass bin in the grocery store downstairs from our apartment, and twice a week a man would come in a truck, bring the potato chips into the store, and dump them in the glass bin. Mama said she didn't want me to have them because there was green mold on them. The chips on the bottom never got to the top. But if they did, I could have them.

At this point I would have eaten all the moldy chips. Every once in a while I would get a penny from Mama's penny jar. I decided to save up $.05. Each time Mama gave me a penny I hid it in my dresser drawer. I couldn't wait to get downstairs to the grocery store. When I saved five pennies, I went into the store and put my $.05 on the counter, and the owner, Mr. Anderson, said, "You can't have those. Your Mama doesn't want you to."

What a disappointment, I thought. I couldn't outsmart Mama. Never! The store also had very good Charlotte Russe which Mama let us have occasionally. I sure wish I had one now. The grocery store didn't have refrigeration for the Charlotte Russe, so when they came into the store we would spread the news by word of mouth, and everyone would come running. I had a yearning for one. The little cakes were placed in white, round cardboard with a whole bunch of whipped cream. As you ate the cream you could push the cardboard up on the bottom, which made the cake come to the top. They tasted so good!

My thoughts drifted back to the little creams that were sold at the candy store. They came in a small tin with a little tin spoon. One day, there was a little girl sitting on the curb with a bag full. Wow! She had red hair and blue eyes and freckles, but I didn't know her name. She looked very cute as she sat there eating her creams. I was kind of a shy boy, but my mouth was watering watching her eating them. So, with all the courage I had, I walked up to her and said, "Can I have one?" and she said, "Yes."

She asked me what color I wanted. They came in pink, yellow, and mint green. I told her I really didn't care, and she handed me a yellow one. I took a walk around the block with it savoring the taste and thinking Mama never got us anything like this. Whenever we asked for anything she thought was a luxury, she would say, "No, we don't have the money for such things." By this time I'd completed my trip around the block. The little red head was still sitting on the curb. I asked for another one, and she gave me a pink one. Then I walked around the block a little faster. Each time I went around the block, I saw a little baby sitting up in his carriage. He was inside the wrought iron gate and his face was so fat. I was tempted to pinch his cheeks, so that's what I did. Of course, the baby cried each time, but those cheeks were so tempting. I was having such a good time walking around the block. I didn't even have to ask for the creams as I passed. She just handed me one each time. About my fourth trip around, the baby's mother caught me and started yelling, "Now I know why my baby's been crying. Get out of here, you hooligan!"

After walking many times around the block, I got so sick I

thought I would throw up. *Gosh, why am I thinking about this now?* I said to myself. I guess all I could think about was food and better times. *Why, oh why is this happening? This isn't what I want; yet I am not stopping myself. What has gotten into me?* I suppose just the thought of surviving was all that was on my mind.

I got up at daybreak and started walking again. My legs were getting very tired, and my wound was pulling a little bit, but I had no choice. If I was going to reach my destination, I had to press on. As I was walking along, this journey started to remind me of something that happened when I was four years old. Mama had put Tony and me into a wicker carriage and walked up to Washington Street, where all the stores were, and then walked all the way down to the end, which was First Street. Then we walked back. It was nice being pushed in a carriage. Mama usually walked with Kitty and her two girls. They were about the same age as my brother and me, and they had their own carriage.

One day when we came home, Mama said she would leave the carriage outside until Papa finished at the butcher. She was never very fond of putting the carriage in the basement because she had to bring it down the steps. She left it there for a short time, and someone took it. This was during the Depression, and carriages were scarce. I remember feeling so upset that my carriage was gone. The next day I saw Bertha outside and told her about the stolen carriage. She said, "You are too big for a carriage anyway. A boy your age shouldn't ride in a carriage." I was devastated. From that time on, my brother and I had to walk until we felt like our legs would fall off.

I did feel like my legs would fall off that day, and I wondered if I would make it. Nights were cold, and the days were a little cool with a fresh breeze. When the sun was out, getting water was always a problem.

As I walked along, my mind continued to wonder back to the days when I was a boy. I remembered a time when Mrs. Ahrens took me to Coney Island and told me a story about when she was a little girl. All of her relatives were scattered around New York, so in the summer time, they would meet at Coney Island beach and exchange used clothing from one child to another. Nothing was ever discarded. She said her mom didn't want to carry bags on the subway, so she would make her wear ten dresses, one on top of the other. She was so warm on a hot, humid summer day. Sometimes when I felt cold, I'd ask myself if I would like to be as hot as Mrs. Ahrens with her ten dresses. At night, I would have liked to be that warm, but it wasn't possible.

I also began thinking of the ocean and all that water when I would get thirsty. I only saw the ocean two times, but it sure was a lot of water. I suppose when you are thirsty you like to think of large bodies of water. I was so homesick and couldn't stop thinking about Kitty and Danny, Mrs. Ahrens, and Kate and Bertha. They were like family to me. We all lived in separate apartments but in one building. Seeing these people every day since I was a youngster had built a strong bond between us. I wondered what they would think of me now. They'd been so proud of me going off in my uniform.

No one drove by until late in the afternoon. I hitched a ride in a U.S. Army jeep with a guy named Mike. He didn't say what his last name was or where he was from. He was very quiet, so I didn't volunteer any information except where I was going and why. He looked at me very strangely and said he didn't know of any U.S.

Army base in Italy. I quickly said, "Well that's what I heard." He said the only base he heard of in Italy was in Casarsa, which was Italian, not American. He took me about thirty miles and never spoke another word to me. I don't think he believed a word I said. When he reached his destination, he let me out and he didn't even say good-bye. I found a spot to spend the night and tried to rest my weary head. I slept intermittently and arose when the sun came up. I didn't realize that I was very close to where I wanted to go, but I didn't want to cross any borders.

I didn't have to wait too long before a guy in an Army truck came along. His name was Nick Tready. He was from New York City and said he was going to a town close to the border. So after three days of walking, riding, and resting as much as I could at night, I made it close to the border. Nick seemed very intent on getting where he was going and not very interested in where I was going or why, and that was fine with me. When he dropped me off, I slowly walked away from the truck with one thought in mind. I had to get rid of this uniform. I had no idea how far it was to my relatives' house on the outskirts of Poffabro. I hoped I didn't have to spend too many nights in the wooded mountains. Nights were the worst because there were all kinds of sounds and animals that were roaming around. It was very cold. There were bombs in the distance, and planes flying over head. I would always tell myself at dusk that this was my rest time, but I could not rest.

I walked for several miles, and off in the distance, I could see a farmhouse. When I arrived there, I saw a farmer outside with a few chickens. I asked him if I could buy a pair of overalls and a top, so I would have something clean to change into. He looked startled and a little frightened of me. He had a little problem communicating, but he knew some words in my dialect, which was Fruilano. He told me that all he had was used and worn clothing. I told him it would be okay because I didn't have much money. He offered to take my uniform in exchange for the clothes. I no longer had any use for the uniform, so I considered it a deal.

Before I left the farm, I asked the farmer if he had any food. He went inside and came out with a slice of brown bread. I knew food was scarce, and I hated to ask, but I was starving. I was eating the bread as I traveled down the road. He watched me guardedly until I left. I still had my gun with me, but now I decided that I must discard it as quickly as I could. Farmers didn't walk around with army guns. I walked about a half-mile threw it into a big ravine.

I needed to be as inconspicuous as I could be. I looked Italian and spoke the language. Without the uniform, I could easily move about. From here on, I had to walk or hitch a ride with a farmer. Even if it was a horse and wagon, it helped. No more military jeeps or trucks.

Whenever I was alone for any length of time, I would be engulfed with homesickness. After I left the farm, I started thinking about the Mary Hammond Home for Children that was a few blocks from where we lived in Hoboken. When I was in grammar school, I met a boy who lived at the Home. His name was Gerard. He told me that he had no one--no mother, father, brothers, sisters, etc. He had only one aunt who couldn't care for him. That's why he was at the Home. He also told me that he could be adopted. I asked Mama if we could take him, and she said, "Sure, at this point, what's one more?" Mama had a big heart and was always feeding the neighborhood kids. She said if the authorities would let us have him that he could come and live with us.

One day we were playing together in the park. They had lavatories for the public to use. I mentioned to Gerard that I was going to go in there. He advised me not to because there were old men in there that did things to little boys. The older boys at the Home told him this. He used very graphic language and words I never heard before.

I felt a bit upset to think that there were people around who would do things like that to children, and that night when Mama tucked me into bed, I told her what he said. She became very excited, and her face flushed. She said it wasn't true and never ever to say those things again. I think I shocked my mother, and she seemed angry. I lost interest in our family adopting Gerard after getting into trouble with Mama over his report about the lavatory. Once or twice, he came to me and said he could be adopted, but nothing ever came of it. I wondered where he was now, if he ever found a home, or if he was as lonely as I am now. I now understood the saying, "Walk a mile in another man's shoes and you'll understand how he feels."

Mama had a friend that lived next door to the Home, and she had a son my age. When we went into her yard, we used to peek through the holes in the big wooden fence and look at all of the orphans. I have no idea why that fascinated me. I suppose there was a little sadness attached to the attraction, knowing that the children didn't have any parents. You could always tell who they were at school. The girls' hair was cut very short, shaved up the back with little pieces of hair half way down on the sides of their ears. They were very unbecoming haircuts, and just when they started to look good, the process started all over again. The boys wore short hair too, but it didn't make as much of a difference as the girls' hair.

I couldn't believe all of these thoughts about the past that kept coming into my head. My whole life was being played in front of me like a movie in the theater. I missed my family with all my heart.

For three or four days I repeated the same routine. I got started early in the morning, walked a lot, and asked the fellows on the vehicles for candy or water. When I found a stream, I filled my canteen with water and tried to use it sparingly because I never knew when I would find the next one. I continued to walk a half a day until I came to another farm. I thought that maybe I could get some water or a piece of bread. When I approached the farm, I noticed all of the animals were loose and the gates were open. I wondered what was going on. I didn't have to wonder for long. As I got closer, I saw a man, woman, and two boys lying on the ground, dead. They had bullet holes in their backs. I should have been used to it from all I had seen, but I wasn't. The only thing I could figure was it must have been political because the soldiers always let the animals out when they came. I was in a quandary. I wanted to ask for bread and water, but here I was staring at four dead bodies. I stood there for ten minutes trying to decide what to do, and then I wondered if he had any papers on him. He sure didn't need them now, but I did. I went over to him and stuck my hand in his pocket and pulled out a billfold. His name was Daniel Corso. There wasn't much money in his billford, but his papers were there with a few bills. I took them both. I felt guilty taking something from a dead man, but he sure didn't have any use for it, not as much as I did. I walked over to the house and opened the door, and on the kitchen table there was about one half of a loaf of brown bread. I took it with me and left.

I started walking again and met a farmer with a horse and wagon and got a ride for as far as he was going. It always helped even if it was for a short distance. It gave my weary legs a rest. I asked the farmer where Poffabro was, and he told me I had to travel by night the rest of my trip to get over the Alps and down into the village. I knew if I could get to my father's relatives in the Italian Alps I could stay with them. When I got to Italy I had to do a lot of walking. When the farmer explained to me where I was in relationship to where I wanted to go, I realized I wasn't too far from my destination. I just had to figure out how I would do this, so I didn't have to go through any checkpoints. It definitely wasn't the easy way, but I went over the mountain and dropped down into Poffabro. My relatives' house was three miles from there on the outskirts of Poffabro in an enclave or cluster called Cudili. Each family estate had several houses on them and had their group of houses named. I just had to find my relatives' house. It was the most difficult part of the trip. I was very exhausted and happy when I reached the town because I knew I would soon be there.

CHAPTER 6

When I walked up to the house, it was very much like the picture I'd seen. The roof was reddish-brown terra cotta and hard kiln-burnt, unglazed clay. Each tile was rounded quite impressively. The house was about one hundred years old but in fairly good condition. The outside walls were fieldstone and stucco, and it had three porches in need of repair. There was a porch that went half way around the house on the first and second floor and outside of the loft on the top floor was another porch. The house had glass windows, no screens, and shutters, which were closed when it got too windy. As I stood and looked at it, I thought, *this is the house where my Papa was born.* I felt very nostalgic. I was a little nervous about how I would be received. I knocked at the door cautiously, and a woman came to the door equally as cautious.

When my aunt opened the door, all she said was, "Yes?" I asked her to stay out on the porch while we talked because I had no idea who was in the house, and I only wanted to talk to her. I also wanted to make sure that she was Aunt Rose. She identified herself, and I told her who I was. I knew as soon as she started talking that she was Dad's sister. She looked liked him, had the same features and coloring, and was also a little robust--not as much as Papa, but I guess they didn't have as much food here as we did in America. I felt the introduction was strained. I tried to explain to her my situation without going into too much detail; and, of course, at this point I did not speak about my new identity. We agreed that she would say I was her cousin from another province of Italy, not from the USA. I told her I remembered the address from the envelopes her letters came in over the years. She never wrote much, but mail from overseas was a big deal as a youngster. I told her I didn't want to impose on them, so I asked if I could stay with them for awhile and do some repairs around the house or work in the fields with our relatives.

They didn't have much. They had even less than Mama and Papa. She explained that after her parents passed away, she barely managed to keep the house going. I asked her where her husband was, and she said, "Come inside, and we will talk some more." When she opened the door, I saw a girl that I presumed was her daughter. There were no big introductions. I came to find out her name was Josephine. Aunt Rose took me into the kitchen. I was surprised to find out that they had no water or electric.

It was a mild day, and the door was open. Chickens were walking in and out looking for some crumbs. Aunt Rose told me to sit down, and she would make some coffee. I looked around the kitchen. There was a sink but no running water. They could put water in the sink to wash dishes, but it ran outside because they had no plumbing. They also had a china closet and a kitchen set. It was a cherry table and a few chairs with rush seats and a bench.

After the coffee was made, she told me her husband was a lumberjack by trade, and he used to get ration coupons to buy sugar, pasta, coffee, and chicory brew. What they couldn't get from coupons, they got from the black market. However, her husband wasn't there because he joined the partisans as part of the underground. I made no comment, just took it all in. As I was drinking my coffee, I kept looking at the stove because it was quite unique and red in color. There was a section for wood that heated the kitchen and was used for cooking and a section for heating water and an oven. The only heat in the house was in the kitchen. She also told me that she worked in a factory that made war parts, tank trucks, etc. She also worked in the fields with the relatives when needed.

Aunt Rose was Dad's sister, but she was nothing like Dad. She wasn't much of a talker; she just said what had to be said and seemed depressed. When we finished our coffee, she showed me the house. Downstairs was the kitchen and two storage rooms. The storage rooms were built into the side of the mountain so they were cool. I was told they were even cool in the summer. In the storage rooms were shelves with food supplies like cheese, salami and Musetto, polenta, and two poles with rope to hang the salami and cheese. We went upstairs and there was no bathroom. The bathrooms in the halls in Hoboken seemed like a luxury at this point.

There were three bedrooms upstairs. Aunt Rose and Uncle Dominick, who was at war, had the largest room. They had light oak furniture, a double bed, two night tables, and a wash stand with a wash basin. The top was marble and the bottom was wood where they could put a few things. There was also a bureau.

Josephine's room had a double bed of light oak with a very large headboard and footboard. She also had a mattress made of corn husks. There was the same type of wash stand and basin as the other room. The third bedroom where I would stay only had a single bed and a bucket for a wash basin. All the beds had feather comforters to keep warm since there was no heat. The Hoboken apartment seemed plush compared to this room. I had to keep reminding myself that this was better than living in a ditch.

They also stored apples and corn kernels in my room. On the top floor was a hayloft used for storage. Outside of the house was the outhouse and well. I didn't bring much with me, only a few things I carried and the clothes on my back, but that was okay because no one else had anything either.

We went back down to the kitchen, and Aunt Rose told me the house schedule. She said, "We all rise early. If you are going to work in the fields, you have to do house errands first." She said this as Josephine walked by with a heavy load, looking like she could use a little help.

The first thing in the morning the cows had to be milked. They had five cows. The milk was picked up by a little paddy wagon pulled by a mule and had to be ready on time. Generally, the cows yielded two full milk pails. The milk was then taken to a co-op they belonged to which was owned and operated by about twenty farmers. When the milk arrived, they would make cheese and divide the cheese amongst the twenty farmers. After the cows were milked, it was time for breakfast.

Josephine prepared most of the meals. She was sixteen years old and had many responsibilities. If her mom was working in the factory, she had to do the milking herself. Otherwise, they would do it together; and when her father was around, he would help. Breakfast consisted of milk and bread. The bread wasn't too good. It was brown bread, all natural, very course, and unbleached. They also drank cafe latte, which was milk with coffee. Polenta was a staple they ate often. This consisted of corn meal. Sometimes they put polenta in milk, which was a little lumpy. The water was boiled, and they put the corn meal in and stirred it for about an hour until it solidified. It was then cooled and sliced.

Then they went to different fields with a scythe and cut grass. The sun would come out and bake the grass dry. Then they flipped it over and dried the other side. When that was done, they made bundles. Many times the bundles were carried down the mountain and placed in a hayloft. Sometimes it was carried on their back in a basket called a *cosc*; other times by rope or on a cable. This was stored for the animals to sleep on in the winter, together with leaves that were raked up.

When they went into the fields, they had to bring lunch with them. Lunch was commonly polenta and cheese. It was about four o'clock when they finished in the field, sometimes a little later. They came back to the house and fed the animals. They had chickens and sold the eggs, but didn't eat them themselves. Every once in a while, Josephine would go to the hen house and find a warm egg, make a hole, and suck out the contents. They had rabbits in big cages and sometimes ate them. There was no meat during the war, so they raised one pig a year and slaughtered it and made salami and Musetto, which was a little like liverwurst but chopped coarsely. The meat was stored in the cool storage rooms of the house.

They had two sheep for the wool. Aunt Rose would spin the wool and make socks, mittens, and sweaters. Josephine could also make something from the wool. They had two goats for the milk and every so often they would mate the cows with the neighbor's bull and then sell off the calves.

Supper was around five or six, depending on how quickly chores were done. Some nights they ate spaghetti, and they spread a little tube of tomato paste on top. The tube looked like toothpaste, and they squeezed it on the spaghetti for flavor. The tomato paste was generally bought from the black market. They also made vegetable soup from the vegetables in the garden and sometimes ate polenta. The one good thing about living on a farm was they could raise their own vegetables and animals. They never wasted anything. Even the cow manure was used to fertilize the garden.

After supper was prayer time. They sat and said the Rosary, and then it was time to go to bed. Since there was no electric, they had to use oil lamps, which they didn't like to burn too long, so they went to bed early. They definitely were very tired. The next day the cycle started all over again. Aunt Rose made it very clear to me that I would be expected to pull my own weight and not be a burden, but a help to them.

May was kind of a rainy month, but nice days were field days. I swept the porch every day and fixed what I could around the house for them. I also worked in the fields. Josephine was the only one I had to talk to. As the days passed by, we grew closer.

She was just four years younger than I was, and she loved to hear stories about America. She said she would love to go to the

USA one day to visit, so I told her as much as I could about our area. When we had our long talks, I would think about Mama and Papa and feel lonely and melancholy. However, I did not write to my parents because I didn't want them to know that I had defected, and I knew that they had probably received an MIA on me. Sometimes I wondered if they believed that I was dead or if they kept believing that I was still alive. I wondered how Papa was doing in the butcher shop, how Tony was, and I thought about the twins. I daydreamed at night when I went to bed about life back in the states.

After I was with Aunt Rose and Josephine for about six months, I started to develop some feelings for Josephine. I was so lonely, and Maria seemed light years away. My life at this point was at an all time low. My memories of the war and defecting didn't allow me to sleep very well. One night, when I was very restless, I arose and went outside to sit on the porch. Josephine heard me and came outside to talk to me. I felt that at this point I had to confide in her. When I confided in Aunt Rose, I never knew if she understood what I was talking about. I told Josephine about my army situation, and just as I thought, she was very understanding and mature beyond her years. Aunt Rose never told anyone what I told her, not even Josephine.

People didn't talk much; everyone was afraid. You just didn't know who you could trust. Fear ruled. After I unburdened myself to Josephine, she said she had a secret to share with me. She said I was not her cousin because Aunt Rose was not her biological mother. She was adopted as a baby. I thought about sharing with Josephine that I had been married, but at that point, I really didn't know if I would even see Maria again. She seemed part of another life. *Would I ever get back to America myself? Would I ever see my family again?* I'd think. Sometimes I thought when the war was over, I would visit my parents briefly and then go to a rural area in upstate New York. I knew I could never live in Hoboken again. I would always have to use my new identity. These were just thoughts. Who knew what the future would bring? As far as Josephine knew, I was a cousin, and due to the atmosphere, not many questions were asked. There were only about three thousand people in that village, so it was a good place to hide.

After talking for many hours, we finally realized that we weren't related. If we hadn't shared our secrets, we would have never known. Josephine was a very plain girl. She had blond hair with a little red in it; I suppose it would be called strawberry blond. She also had light green eyes, and her hair was long, but she kept it braided or just pulled back. She had a medium build and wasn't too tall. Josephine also had a hooked nose. I guess that was an Italian trademark, as Papa had a nose just like that. Her lips were perfect, and I couldn't help but look at them. Overall, she had a very pleasant face with a calm demeanor, so easy to be with. She was shy and pleasant. The girls in the Italian Alps were untouched by the world--no makeup, no glamour. They were very plain.

Josephine wore a blue cotton housedress almost everyday. On Saturday night, she would wash it and hang it in the kitchen to dry, so she could wear it to church on Sunday. She also wore scalletti, which were basically wooden shoes on the bottom with leather tops. Her father made her shoes with little nails to hold the leather on the wood.

Shoes were sometimes made from old tires. They would cut a sole from the rubber and make a velvet top with little pompoms, or else they would use cloth. Josephine never wore a scarf on her head, but Aunt Rose always had one. It was something the older women did. There were some things I didn't think I would ever get used to. Some older women didn't wear underwear. When they had to urinate, they would just walk down the rode, lift their long skirt a bit, and do it right on the side of the rode. It would run down their legs and they would just keep walking. All you had to do was come within three feet of these women to really smell them. You knew they were there!

It was very different being here than being with my family at home. I felt that the relationship was always strained with Aunt Rose. All of their customs were different. I tried to talk to Josephine about it and she said, "That's just the way she is. We speak the same language but we're so different. She has had a very hard life."

I questioned Josephine about going to school. There was a little schoolhouse about two blocks from the house that the village children went to. They only attended from age five until age ten, which meant kindergarten to fifth grade. If they wanted more education, they had to go to a city. Of course, some children never had the opportunity to go at all. It was a one-room schoolhouse, and one teacher taught all the grades.

Josephine said all of the kids were given castor oil at school for worms. Many children had dry scaly skin from lack of vitamins. School was not fun for Josephine. The teacher was strict and punished the children by placing them in the corner or hitting them with a switch. Children attended from October to June so they could help harvest the crops.

Most children had to help on the farms. I couldn't help compare all we had in America to their way of living. It seemed like two different worlds, and it was. Josephine would not believe what she saw in America if she ever had the opportunity to visit.

Josephine also picked mushrooms. Sometimes she worked all day and then tried to sell them to the neighbors, but she was not a salesgirl. When she went from door to door to sell them, everyone would say, "Oh, I got mine already." She was very demure and would just walk away. Then Aunt Rose would go out and have to sell them. The same thing would happen in the fall when they picked up chestnuts. She would go out and get them and never have any customers to buy them. Josephine had a hard life. When she brought water into the house, she would use a water yolk around her neck with two poles out to the side with the buckets of water. I wonder what she would say if she saw Mama's sink with the copper faucets and running water. She would think she'd died and gone to heaven.

Josephine was a very good girl and went to church every Sunday. She had to go into the village of Poffabro where St. Nichols Church stood. It was three miles away, and most of the time, she walked. Sometimes she took her bike. The outside of the church looked like white sandstone, and it had a big bell tower. The inside was all marble, and it was very beautiful. There was a man called Beppi Solar who rang the church bells every day. Everyone used to say he was homeless because he always begged, but he really wasn't. He had a small home passed down through his family, but he continued to beg and smelled very bad. Beppi was always part of the town gossip.

Josephine and I talked until almost dawn, and both of us were talked out and tired. She leaned towards me to place her hand on mine, and I kissed her. It was a light brotherly kiss. I surprised myself, and I quickly recovered but was haunted by her touch. After all, even though she seemed older, she was only sixteen years old.

The next morning at breakfast, she kept looking at me for some type of confirmation. She fixed polenta for breakfast, and we ate in silence. I avoided her eyes as she kept looking at me. I didn't know what I was feeling myself. Another week went by and then something happened again. This time I couldn't deny my feelings. I was falling in love with her.

We talked every day and made plans about going to America when the war was over. I knew I couldn't get divorced, but I was blocking that out. Maybe I could marry with my new identity. However, then I would be a bigamist. I knew I was blocking out what I didn't want to face. It really is strange how we can rationalize everything in our life that we want to as long as it fits in with our plans. I have come so far from Mama and Papa's teaching. Sometimes I wonder where this will all end. All I knew was that I wanted Josephine to come to America with me. I wanted to show her all of the things I told her about. Time kept moving forward, and I had now been there eight months.

I asked Aunt Rose if I could get a job in the factory where she worked. She said she would ask for me. I told her I would use the papers I had taken from the dead man at the farm. By that time, I had told her about how I obtained the papers. She came home from work that day and said they could use some help and that I could start the next day.

Josephine had started supper. She was making spaghetti

when a knock came at the door. We looked out and saw some soldiers. We knew they were the S.S. About six soldiers came in, and the rest stayed outside. I got up from the table and slipped into the closet. As of yet, no soldiers had questioned me. They wanted to know where Aunt Rose's husband was, with the partisans. Aunt Rose said she didn't know, and that was the truth. She really knew nothing.

The soldiers felt she was resisting so they started to brutally beat her trying to get information from her. All she could do was cry and tell them that she didn't know. I never saw a person beaten that badly, and all I could do was watch. I felt terrible. I had no weapons and even if I did, how could I stand up against them? After they left, Aunt Rose was in a great deal of pain. We comforted her as much as we could, gave her a little supper. and put her to bed. The next morning her back was all black and blue, but she still had to go to work. She could not afford to stay home.

The S.S. Italian soldiers were the ones that were affiliated with Hitler. Some soldiers went with the Nazis, and some went with the partisans. Josephine's father chose the latter. The S.S. would come at night, set fires, let the animals out, beat people up, and get people to turn on each other.

The German planes were overhead every day. They did not occupy the area; they just passed through and caused trouble. One time a bomb was dropped on top of the mountain by mistake. Aunt Rose and Josephine thought that surely it was the end. It was so frightening never knowing what each day would bring. There was heavy bombing ten miles from the house. You could hear it all the time. I was glad I was going to work with Aunt Rose, so I could keep an eye on her.

We left for the factory in the morning. Most families only had one bicycle, but Aunt Rose and Josephine had two because they traded one for an animal, so I was able to use Josephine's bike to go to the factory. We had to ride five miles to Moniago. The beauty of the mountains and how well manicured they were never ceased to amaze me. It looked like pictures of Switzerland I had seen as a child. It's a good thing Aunt Rose made me a heavy sweater for winter and gave it to me for Christmas because it was cold. Josephine made me a hat and mittens. Riding those bikes up some of those hills kept our blood circulating.

Aunt Rose had some bruises on her face, but she was able to cover the rest of the marks on her body. She never complained on our ride there. She just did what she had to do. When we arrived, I was introduced to the foreman. Other than asking for my papers, there were no questions. I showed my papers and didn't volunteer any information. The only thing they wanted was my present address, which I gave them. Everyone there was very adept at minding their own business for their own good health.

Every Monday was a street market in Moniago. You could get all of the supplies that you needed. Each day they set up in a different town. They carried everything the local store didn't have. We could buy leather, clothes, food, spices, etc., so we would purchase what we could carry home on the bicycle. For the next year and a half, we worked in the factory and in the fields. Sometimes I was able to save a little money.

Josephine and I grew very close, and we shared everything. It was now two years since I had arrived. Josephine had blossomed into a beautiful woman. Our love grew stronger. Times together were always sweet, not that we had much time alone. We were close but not intimate.

We kissed and held hands and talked about our future. She was so innocent and believing. In times of war, most people only think of living for the day, for who knows what tomorrow may bring. It was our hope of being together that kept us going. Even if we made plans that never came to pass, we enjoyed the moment of making the plans. Every day was a like day, and the pleasure of her company made it bearable.

In the summer of 1945, the news came that the war was over. I knew I could go back to America but not home to live. I was desperately hoping that the authorities wouldn't catch up with me. Josephine and I had many talks about what would happen when the war ended, so when I told her that I was going to sail back on the Conte Biancamno, she wasn't surprised, but she was apprehensive. As the days flew by to my departure date, she became very petulant. All of the "what if's" started coming. I had to reassure her dozens of times that when I got settled, I would send for her. She agreed but felt that an ocean between us was just too far. When it was time for me to leave, there were tears, promises, and lots of hugs. I told her that we would be together soon, that she would just have to trust me, and that I would honor my promises to her. The day I left, she came to see me off, and I had a strange feeling of deja vu. I started doubting myself, and when I got on the ship, I had to put down all of the thoughts that hit me at once--Maria, Mama, Papa, my AWOL status. I hadn't kept very many promises in the last few years, but the one I promised myself, with all that was in me, was that I would bring Josephine to America.

CHAPTER 7

The day I sailed was a nice day in late fall of 1945. I stood at the rail and waved to Josephine for as long as we could see each other. I wrote her a poem and asked her to open it when the ship pulled out. Tears streamed down her face like the soft trickle of a gentle rainfall while she read the poem:

Now is the time when we must part,
But I will always have you in my heart.
I love you today, and I'll love you tomorrow.
My heart is heavy and filled with sorrow.
Josephine, you have become such a part of my life,
Leaving you has brought me such strife.
This ship will soon be headed out to sea,
And I ask, "Please remember me."

The feelings I expressed in the poem meant a lot to me. I watched Josephine's lips tremble as she softly read the words aloud. As I gazed at her from the ship, I hoped she could feel the love I had for her. I hoped she would wait for me and remember me and continue to love me. All we had now was our promises to each other, and I hoped it would last. When we could no longer see each other, I went to my cabin. It was dark and dingy with two bunk beds, but I had to make the best of it. I preferred to stay on deck, as the sunshine and the sound of the water lifted my spirits.

The trip was quite uneventful. I had roommates, but we didn't speak to each other very much. I stayed out of the room as much as I could, so I wouldn't have to talk to anyone. I am sure they thought I was anti-social. The weather was fair with two rough days. All the more reason I wanted to be upstairs. When I needed some air, I went out for a few minutes. I couldn't stay out too long because it was very cold.

After being at sea for a day or two, I started to think about what I would say to Papa. He didn't know if I was dead or alive. I knew that he was going to be very disappointed in me. Papa had such high hopes for me, and I thought this would devastate him. I would have a lot of explaining to do about the Army and most of all about Josephine. We were good Catholics and believed in "until death do us part." Maybe he would feel so disgraced, he would have found it easier to accept the fact that I died than hear this news. I couldn't deny what happened or my feelings for Josephine. I couldn't make up something that didn't exist to satisfy Papa. I had to tell him everything. It was now two and a half years since they had heard from me. Would they be glad to see me? Ashamed? Disenchanted? Whatever happened, I had to face my destiny. After ten days, the ship arrived in New York.

I planned on getting to the house around 11 p.m. as there would be less of a chance of running into someone I knew. I had grown a beard and combed my hair differently. But how different could I look? If people thought I was dead, they certainly wouldn't be looking for me. At 11 o'clock, I knocked on the door quietly. Papa opened the door, and Mama came right behind him. They knew who I was instantly. My big disguise didn't fool them. They both smothered me in tears and hugs and said they always hoped I would be alive. Mama said it was her faith that had kept her going.

I told them that I knew it was late, but I had to talk to them that night because there was so much to tell. We sat at the kitchen table, and I took a deep breath. We had to talk low so as not to wake the others. I told them first about the Army. I was as honest as I could be about what happened. Papa got very emotional. I felt like I was tearing his heart out. I was his firstborn son. He was so proud of me. How could this be? They were both very upset. Mama kept wiping her tears on her apron. Papa was more upset than she was. He looked like someone had died. I guess something did die inside of him. His American dream of having his son serve the country he had come to love was gone.

Mama excused herself and went to bed. I said, "Papa, there is more. I don't know how much you can take, but I have to tell you everything." Papa said, "Let me put on some coffee, and we can talk." There was so much to say and so little time.

Papa knew what kind of trouble I would be in if I got caught and how dangerous it was for me to even be at the apartment, but he also knew that this may be the last time we could meet and much needed to be said. Papa placed two cups of strong coffee on the table. I began to tell him about Josephine, how I met her and fell in love with her and wanted to marry her. I explained how I thought she was my cousin only to find out that she was adopted. Papa became ghastly white as I brought forth all of the information. I became a little frightened and hoped that I would not give Papa a heart attack or stroke. Papa kept shaking his head and saying, "No, you can't do that, you are already married." I then proceeded to tell him about my new identity and plan for a new life.

This was all too much for papa. The AWOL and the Josephine story totally overwhelmed him. Papa sat there for ten minutes without saying anything. I thought he was thinking about all of the things that he was going to say to me about how I had ruined his life and reputation. Instead, my father had a rather humble look on his face and said, "Joe, you cannot marry Josephine. This has got to be the hardest thing I ever had to tell you. I know how much you have always looked up to me, but you can never marry Josephine because she is your sister. In 1927, after Tony was born, we left for America. I had a brief affair with Josephine's mother. She was six months pregnant when we came to America. My sister, your Aunt Rose, took Josephine from her mother at birth and raised her as her own since she never had any children. I sent money whenever I could to help them out. This is one of the things I am not proud of in my life. I hope you can forgive me."

"Papa, sometimes we don't know who we are until we are tried and tested. I think about what my life would have been like with Josephine. What would my life have been like if I had stayed in the Army? What would my life have been like had I stayed true to myself? Some things we will just never know."

Now it was my turn to be dismayed. I was speechless and

heartbroken. All that could be heard within our kitchen was the sounds of my uncontrollable sobbing.

When I composed myself, I said, "Well, Papa I can't stay here. I had hoped to bring Josephine here and move to upstate New York in a very rural area and have some kind of a life, but I see now that can't be." Papa said his brother's son, Nicolas, took an interest in Maria and since everyone thought I was dead, Maria started to go on with her life after a brief mourning period. After all, she was a young girl, too, and had to have some kind of life.

"Nicolas is going to be engaged to Maria in November," said Papa.

"Papa, not that I could go back to Maria anyway, but I will now know the true meaning of loneliness. I truly am a man without a country. I didn't have an honorable discharge. I am a man without a family. I may never see Mama and you again. Even though I've changed my appearance, someone may recognize me. I am a man without a friend. I left Austria because I was lonely and homesick, and now I am still lonely and homesick. I will never have the privilege of having Sunday dinner with the family or visiting with my aunts, uncles, cousins and friends, even with my neighbors at 252-11th Street. Oh, God, what have I done? What have I done?"

"Joe, there is more to tell you. I am sorry that your last visit here is going to be so sad, but you have to know. After you left, your brother, Tony, helped me with the butcher shop. The meat wasn't good; it was very tough. Meat was scarce, and everyone had to use the ration coupons. Business was poor. In the mean time, Rosalie Gracomo got pregnant, and they had to get married. She was three months pregnant when they married and that was seventeen months ago. They had no money and needed an apartment, baby furniture, and clothing for the baby. He worked nights at the shipyard. That way he wouldn't have to worry about being drafted. Sometimes, he worked 3 to 11, and sometimes he worked 11 to 7. He also had some friends that worked on the docks, and they told him to go down to the piers and shape up. He knew the boss loader on Pier 4, Jim Monte. Jim was an acquaintance of his so he went down to the docks to stand in line to shape up for work."

"So he stood in long lines with lots of other guys waiting to be selected for work as a longshoreman for the day?"

"Yes. When there was no work, he helped me in the butcher shop. When he didn't come, I worked alone. The dock job worked out for awhile, and then there was some talk about forming a union, which Tony may have been involved in."

"Tony, involved in a union?"

"I don't know. There are lots of rumors. I can't say if there was any truth to the union story. What I do know is that Tony was a good worker and was getting very aggravated when he was getting shut out and not getting picked. Apparently, he and Jim Monte had a confrontation, which led to a big fight at the Blue Lagoon Tavern on River Street. It was around 8:30 in the evening on August 27th. It must have been a very bad fight because Tony was enraged.

"Tony's temper will flare if he is pushed."

"Tony only went to the tavern to confront Jim, but it turned ugly. Jim Monte was a very tough guy with a record a mile long. Jim Monte served ten years in prison for almost every crime imaginable."

"And I bet there are some he never served time for," I said.

"He was also on trial for another murder but didn't get convicted. He was a hoodlum. He held the contracts for work on the docks. Who knows what you had to do to get work?"

"Papa, do you think Tony ever did something he shouldn't have?"

"I don't know why Tony felt he needed a gun except for the fact that he knew Jim had one. When he left the tavern after the brawl, the police think he went looking for a gun and went back to the tavern some time after 10 p.m. There is much that is unclear in all of this, but Tony was found dead on the sidewalk outside of the tavern. The police said that his skull had been crushed and he'd been shot behind the right ear."

I immediately grabbed my chest, and I felt like my lungs were going to explode. The news of my brother's death crushed my chest like a vise. After a few minutes, I started crying and felt like I couldn't stop. The shock of hearing my brother was dead was so overwhelming. It was sucking the life and breath out of me. I was trying very hard to hold in my sobs so that I would not wake the twins.

Papa kept rubbing my back and talking softly to me, but I knew the shock of this news was too much for me to bear. I finally asked, "What about Rosalie?"

"She went back to her parents' apartment because she couldn't afford to live alone and take care of the baby. She had a little girl and named her Antoinette. Her mother takes care of the baby, and she works at the ice cream parlor across the street. Believe me, Joe, the hardest thing I ever had to do was to go to her apartment with her father and give her this news. Two patrolmen came to our door about 11 p.m. Mama and I had just gone to bed when I heard someone knocking at the door. I put my robe on and went into the kitchen. I asked who it was before opening the door. The men identified themselves as patrolmen and gave their names. By this time Mama had gotten out of bed, put her robe on, and came into the kitchen. I opened the door and the two officers stepped inside. I couldn't imagine what they wanted. They asked us to sit down on our chairs at the kitchen table, and we did. Then they broke the news. It all happened so fast that our heads were spinning. They stayed a little while and told us what they knew, which wasn't much. The whole thing had to be investigated. They offered their condolences and said if we needed anything to contact them. We were numb. Neither one of us could feel."

"How did Mama deal with this whole thing?"

"Mama had to lie down right away and I got her a cold rag for her head. I felt very hot. I think my blood pressure went up. My heart was beating fast, and I felt weak. I was trying my best to take it all in, but it just wasn't registering. Mama called from her bed and asked me to go tell Rosalie, but I said I thought we should wait until morning. Then she said that bad news travels fast, and Rosalie might hear it from someone else first or on the radio. I didn't want to leave Mama because she was in rough shape, but at that hour I didn't want to disturb anyone else or tell this news to anyone. It was all I could do to digest this and make myself function. This was a nightmare to end all nightmares."

Papa got up from his chair and began pacing the floor as if he was reliving the whole horrible event again. "I got dressed and went around the corner to the Gracomo's apartment and broke the news to Rosalie's parents. It was another devastating scene.

After Rosalie's father composed himself, we went up to Rosalie's fourth floor apartment to tell her. It was about 12:30 a.m., and we were having a terrible heat wave. I thought we might wake her up, but she was sitting by the window trying to get some air, waiting for Tony to come home. She had toxemia and was all blown up with fluid."

"She was always so tiny."

Papa began to rub the back of his head. "It was a heart wrenching experience having to tell her. I think she woke up everyone in the building with her screams. At one point, I thought we were going to lose her. Her face and neck and chest were beet red. She was crying and screaming uncontrollably and sweating profusely. She had Tony's slippers on and a huge housedress wrapped around her that she had borrowed from her mother. It was the most pathetic scene I have ever experienced in my whole life."

"Papa, sit down."

Papa hung on to the chair as if he needed the strength to hold himself up. He lowered himself into the chair very slowly. "We now have a little granddaughter that we see frequently, but it is a very bittersweet experience. We love her and see Tony's face in hers every time we look at her. The memory will always be there."

After the initial shock wore off, I wanted the details of what happened. Papa said, "As I told you before, much of it is unclear. The details are sketchy."

"I want to know."

"There were six longshoremen in the tavern. Two of the guys were shot. Jim Monte was shot in the leg and George Stott was shot in the arm. They weren't hurt badly. They were released from

St. Mary's Hospital after they were treated."

"Were the police involved?"

"Oh, yes! They questioned many of the people at the tavern, but no one would talk. They all said that they neither saw nor heard anything."

"I don't believe that!"

"Chief Hogart and his assistant questioned everyone who was there, but everyone remained silent."

"Why?"

"I don't know. It was evident that there were shots fired. Ed Lehman, the owner of the tavern, denied even hearing any shots."

"Do you think they were paid off?"

"It's possible. The cops arrived at about 10:30 p.m. They didn't know about the fight that took place earlier at the tavern. A cop on duty in a police car called for backup from the police box when he heard the shots."

"Isn't it amazing that a cop in a police car heard the shots, but no one in the tavern did?"

"They claimed the music was playing too loud in the tavern to hear anything going on outside. According to the police, Jim Monte and George Stott were running from the door of the tavern towards the piers when the cops stopped them. Jim Monte was taken in the police car to the hospital and George was taken by ambulance. The other men were sitting at the end of the bar when Chief Hogart entered."

"And no one said they saw anything?"

"They all played dumb! Since no one would talk, the police put the pieces together themselves and filed charges against Jim Monte."

"He should fry!"

"Even the cook that worked at the tavern was questioned. He said he didn't see anything. The paper said that two pistols had been used, but only one .38 caliber revolver was found. Captain Hogart found the gun hidden beneath a loose board in a gazebo behind the tavern in the yard."

"Why do you think Tony went back to the tavern?"

"I am not sure. When he went back to the tavern, he walked into a loaded situation. The fight started again and possibly some of the others took part. The police think they hit Tony with the butt of a gun, and then the shooting started."

"Tony should have never gone back."

"After the shooting, Tony tried to leave the tavern, and he collapsed outside a few feet from the entrance. They cleaned up the evidence, and then Jim and Ed ran out only to be caught by the police."

"Why did Tony have to go back?"

"I wish he would have never gone back. Maybe he would still be here today. Captain Hogart also discovered a sleeve torn from Jim's shirt tucked under another board in the gazebo. The cook had to see someone go through, because the gazebo was right behind the kitchen."

"Maybe they threatened him. Maybe he was afraid for his own life."

"I think they threatened to bump him off. Whoever hid the gun had to go through the kitchen when the cook was there. Tony was shot behind the ear, so the police thought the bullet came from behind the bar. The bullets that hit Tony and George were also recovered but not the gun. All of the men except Jim were charged with conspiracy to conceal and obstruct justice."

"This is unbelievable!"

"As soon as word got out about Tony's death, the cousins from downtown got together with some friends, found some guns, and went out looking for Jim Monte. They were going to kill him. He wasn't kept in the hospital very long because his wound wasn't serious. He was immediately sent to jail when he was released from St. Mary's Hospital. It wasn't long before we heard that Jim hung himself. Even that story is debatable. My cousin was working at St. Mary's Hospital as a nurse, and she was taking care of a longshoreman. He told her the cops beat him up and that he didn't hang himself. We will never know."

"He got what he deserved."

"All we know is that Jim is dead. He was to go on trial next month. He was under a federal indictment naming him and several others for conspiracy to avoid payment of a lot of money in Internal Revenue taxes on alcohol by operating two large stills in the Pocono Mountains. He should never have been allowed out of prison because trouble followed him wherever he went."

"Papa, I wish I could have been here to help you and Mama through all of this tragedy."

"This is very overwhelming for both of us. I have tried to give you and your brother the best upbringing I could. I know I was very idealistic, maybe too much sometimes. Maybe you two couldn't live up to my ideals, but I wanted the American dream for all of us. Surely I missed the mark myself. Many times I regretted leaving Italy and my daughter, Josephine. "

"She is very beautiful, Papa. Josephine is a kind and good woman. You would be very proud of her."

"I knew that she didn't have what she should have had. When I looked at the twins, I thought about her and what she was doing and what her life was like. I made a mistake. You made a mistake. Tony made a mistake, and God forgives us. There is forgiveness, but there are always consequences to wrong doing. You must learn to forgive yourself, as I have had to do. It's not easy and it doesn't come quickly, so in the end we suffer for our wrongdoing."

"Do you think God forgives me, Papa?"

"God forgives all who ask, but we must live with the pain we create. I lost my two sons. You are as good as dead. I hope you never get caught. It would be a fate worse than death to go to prison for desertion, so you will suffer for the rest of your life and be separated from your family. My hope and blessing for you would be that you would marry and have children and start a new life. I know it can't include us. I want to give you Tony's leather jacket that he wore down at the docks. It will be cold in New York State in the winter. You may need it."

As Papa handed me the jacket, I looked it over carefully. It was dark tan with some black dirt spots on it, and it was peeling in spots. I took the jacket, placed it against my face, and smelled it. "Papa, I feel like Tony is still here. I feel like when we slept on the studio couch in the parlor. This jacket smells like Tony. Papa, I will never throw the jacket out. I love you and Mama and Tony so much. My heart is broken for what I did. If I could do it over again, I would do it differently, so you could be proud of me, and I could hold my head high instead of sneaking around in the middle of the night to see you. I love my sisters and will never see them get married or have children. This has to be the saddest day of my life."

By then, Papa was crying and he said, "Joe, I love you. There is nothing you could ever do that would make me stop loving you. I am not happy about what you did but neither are you, so go in peace now, and God be with you in your new life. I'll love you always."

As we embraced, I kept repeating, "What have I done? What have I done?" As I walked down the stairs, all of the memories from my youth came flooding back. When I opened the door to walk away, I knew this was forever. I would never be back. Walking down the street in the dark, I quietly said good-night and good-bye to Hoboken and all of my family and friends.

CHAPTER 8

When I left my parent's apartment, I walked to the train in Weehawken. It was a long walk but there weren't any buses running at that hour, and it felt good to be out in the fresh air. I wanted to get the first train out of Weehawken to Phoenicia, New York. I knew there were some trains that went directly to Phoenicia and some that went to Kingston where you had to change trains. I really didn't care which one I took as long as I could get out of Hoboken quickly. I didn't want to be seen or run into anyone I may have known. It was a cool night as some nights can be in the fall, but the walk would do me good with all of my pent up emotions. I thought the walk would help relieve some of my stress.

As I walked, I thought back over my whole life. I thought about Mama and Papa and the butcher shop, our relatives in downtown Hoboken, and Maria. I wondered if she would marry my cousin Nicolas. They didn't seem like a suitable couple to me, but when you are lonely, you do a lot of things differently--not that my cousin wasn't a nice guy. He was a wonderful person, but he just was not for Maria. I couldn't put too much thought into that because at this point my life was over with her. I had an emptiness that just couldn't be filled with my own thoughts. I had best be thinking about my new life, where I would establish myself with my new identity and try to build a life for myself. It can't be the same. It definitely won't be, but I have got to try to make a new life. It was taking all of the effort I have to push myself to go on. I'd just as soon curl up in a corner somewhere and not do anything, but that wasn't possible either.

When I arrived at the station, I had to wait a couple of hours. I planned to take the first train out that morning. The first train was 8:00 a.m. During ski season, the trains left a little earlier, but ski season didn't start yet. Many skiers took the train up to New York for the weekend, but you had to be into the sport and have the money for it. Most of the people I knew didn't have that kind of money, which was good for me, because I certainly didn't want to run into anyone I knew. *Dear God*, I thought. *Will I spend the rest of my life running and hiding?*

Since I had some time to wait, I looked around and found a very small diner, which was barely lit. I stopped and had some coffee. I was starting to get very tired, but I didn't want to fall asleep in the train station. I knew I could sleep a little on the train, and I certainly didn't want to miss the train, so I got some strong coffee.

I sat in the station imagining what it would be like in upstate New York and what I would do for a living. I supposed all of the pieces would fall into place when I arrived there. I closed my eyes for a little while and must have drifted off to sleep because when I awoke, I only had five minutes until the train arrived. I looked around cautiously to see if I knew anyone, and I didn't. I really didn't expect to bump into anyone, but you never knew who would be lurking just around the corner. I got my ticket, and I was on the train that went directly to Phoenicia. I was glad that I didn't have to change trains. I was only there once, and I hardly remembered the place, but it stuck in my mind how quaint and homey it was. Since I did not have a family at this time, this quaint, small town appealed to me.

The ride was quite uneventful. I slept most of the way, and in spite of all of the stops we made, we arrived around noon. I had a small bag with me that contained all of my belongings, which wasn't much. The train stopped up by the bridge by the woodlands, and I walked into town. The town was very small but had most of the conveniences. There wasn't anything you couldn't get if you needed it. The larger town of Kingston was 25 miles away, but this would suit me fine.

As I walked down the street, I noticed a drug store and two hotels, the Phoenicia Hotel and the Gracley Hotel. There was a market with a post office inside, a general store, and a small movie theatre. I walked up to the movie theatre and noticed they had a film each night, and in the summer, they were open every day. They had an early and late movie. I saw a clothing store, which the drugstore also owned; a barber shop, a hardware store, and an old-time diner. There was a gas station, auto repair, a very small Baptist Church, and a Catholic Church on Main Street. The Catholic Church was a few blocks down from the main part of town with only the funeral home and a few residents in that area. There was also a restaurant in town, and I noticed there were two gas stations. One was an old time replica of the Alamo. They had a flying A with wings on it called Title A. Just down the block from the movie house was a Methodist Church. I was quite impressed. For a little town, they certainly had everything. It gave me a great feeling to know that this would be home for a long time. I liked it. I sensed this place would be good for me.

After touring the small town, my thoughts turned to work. What kind of work would I apply for? I thought of the market because I had experience, but I thought better of that. Someone might see me, so I decided to go to the Gracely Funeral Home and see if they needed a handy man. The man who owned the place was very nice. This was real small town business where a handshake sealed most agreements. I didn't want to walk into the front door just in case someone was having a viewing, so I knocked on the back door and a very friendly gentleman came to the door and introduced himself. He said his name was Don Gracely. He shook my hand and asked how he could help me. I told him I was looking for work and asked if he needed help. To my surprise, he said he was looking for a handyman who could clean, make repairs, and help by accompanying him to pick up some of the deceased from the hospitals, nursing homes, or private homes. He asked if I felt I could do that. I said yes and was grateful for the opportunity. I thought it would be much harder to find work, and this was certainly an answer to prayer.

Don was a very warm and helpful individual. I told him I needed a place to stay, and he sent me to a little place right outside of town that was within walking distance. He said, "Before you leave, let me give you a tour of my place and show you around." He took me inside and showed me the viewing room and the embalming room (which I wouldn't have anything to do with).

The place was very clean and cozy, and had a great deal of warmth from Don. I was to vacuum every day, dust, clean the bathrooms, mow the lawn, tend to the bushes and flowers, and maintain the outside of the house next door that Don lived in with his wife and children. I knew right away the kind of person Don was. He told me he always helped the widows with their finances and gave all their husbands a decent burial regardless of how much money they had. He was a real family man and went to Mass every day. Don was kind-hearted and helpful to everyone in the community. I could tell as people strolled in and out that he was held in high esteem.

After my tour, I set out to the little cottage that Don recommended. I was so glad it wasn't far from town. It was less than a half mile. The sign outside said 'Tom's Cabins.' I knocked on the door, and a little man with gray hair man came out and introduced himself. He said his name was Tom. I told him I would be working for Don, and he welcomed me. He showed me the little cabin. I thought it was a hunting cabin because it was very plain. The outside was brown wood siding with cream color trim and shutters. It had a very small porch and two rocking chairs. When I opened the door, I entered into a kitchen-living room combination. The kitchen was very small but adequate. I opened the cabinets, and they had dishes, glasses, pots, utensils and dishtowels. There was a small stove and refrigerator. The living room had a studio couch and one rocking chair with cushions and a little table and lamp. There was one bedroom across the back with a double bed and maple dresser and a bathroom with a tub, sink, and toilet. They supplied towels. I was ecstatic! The rent was reasonable, and I paid for the first month.

I put my little bag down, looked around, and said to myself, "This is home!"

By this time, I was getting hungry, so I walked back to town to get some groceries. I realized that each day I would have to shop before coming home because I couldn't carry too much. At some point, maybe, I could buy a cart or a second hand bike and that would help. As I walked back to town, I stood across the street from where I would be working. Both buildings were very well groomed, white with black shutters and black trim. I hoped I could do a good job and not mess up. I really needed this job, and I couldn't afford to lose it. I would give it my best tomorrow and see what happens.

The next morning I arose early and started my new job. I didn't want to be late, so I arrived about one-half hour early. I did my chores just like I was told, and Don invited me next door for lunch. I met his wife and children that weren't in school yet. In some way, he reminded me of Papa. He was very hospitable. The afternoon went by pretty quickly, and before I knew it, it was time to leave. I went to the grocery store, got some food, and went home. There was a little radio in the cabin, which was nice. I could listen to music, get some news and listen to some stories. It didn't get too many stations, but it was nice to have anyway.

As time went on, I settled into a routine. I went to early Mass on Sunday because there wasn't many people. I occasionally went to the movies but that is about all that I did. I didn't want to get too friendly with people for fear of questions, and I didn't want to keep lying for fear I would forget what I said.

Christmas came and went. Don invited me to spend Christmas at his house, but aside from Don, I didn't have any friends. Life was lonely. I read some books, listened to the radio, and went to the movies. That was it. I was busy with my job and eventually became more like family to Don and his children. In the cold weather, Don would let me drive his car home, so I didn't have to walk home in all the snow and ice.

About a year passed, and all was well except the evenings and weekends when there was no work. As long as I was working, I wasn't thinking, but on Sunday my conscience would bother me. My loneliness would hurt me, and my misgivings would etch into the very being of my soul. I began talking to myself *Can I live with this? Can I ever forgive myself? This isn't really living; it's only existing. To think of spending the rest of my life like this is simply maddening. I need someone to talk to before I lose my mind.*

The following Saturday, I went to confession and told the priest what I had done. He asked me if I was sorry. I told him words could not express how sorry I was, and if I could do it over, I would do it differently, but I couldn't. "What should I do?"

He said, "If you are truly sorry, God forgives you, and now you must forgive yourself." He gave me some prayers to say, and I left.

When I reached home, I kept saying to myself, *How does one forgive himself? I want to do this over. I want to do it right. How do I start?*

The seasons were changing quickly, and before I knew it, the fall was here again. I was grateful for my job and the people I worked for. They were wonderful to me, but I couldn't get rid of the ache in my heart. Thinking about the holidays coming up even made me sadder. I was always thankful that Don didn't pry into my life. He noticed that I was hesitant to talk about the past, and he didn't pursue it. That was a blessing. I didn't have to keep telling more and more lies.

One Saturday night before Thanksgiving, I was finished with work a little early. I went to a phone booth and called Papa at the butcher shop. I knew I was taking a chance, but I just had to hear his voice. When he heard me on the other end, he said, "Hold on, I'll lock the door. I was just finishing up, and this way I can talk without interruptions. Papa was so excited to hear from me. I told him about my job and my life, which wasn't much, and my loneliness. I asked him about Maria, and he said she didn't marry my cousin, Nicolas. They called off the engagement, and she was still working in the five-and-ten cent store and living downtown. I asked him where she was living, and he gave me her address. He also told me Maria's mother had died, and she was having a hard time grieving. We said our good-byes, and I told him I didn't know when or if I would call again and to give my love to Mama. Our conversation ended on a sad note. What else could we say? We certainly couldn't say, "See you soon."

For the next couple of weeks, I did nothing but think about Maria. I thought about my love for her. I thought about her loneliness with her mother gone. They were so close. I thought about our life together, how much we loved each other, and our plans for the future and our wedding. I missed her terribly. The feelings I had for Josephine were brotherly fondness coupled with loneliness. I never had the feelings for Josephine that I had for Maria. My thinking grew into obsession. All I could do was think about her day and night, about what kind of life we might have, or if she would even want me now. I lied and deceived her—she thinks I am dead—then I show up and expect her to join me in this deceptive life? I just don't know.

This is what I want, but can this be? The turmoil grew in me day by day. I know I am being selfish to ask her to do this, but I also know I cannot go on like this indefinitely. I am not free to marry anyone else. I made a vow to her on our wedding day. I began praying, "Lord, help me, what should I do?"

The week before Christmas I was overwhelmed with emotion. I knew this was crazy, but I decided to write to her and tell her how I felt about her and ask her if she still cared for me. I asked God to help me to write this letter.

Dear Maria,

First of all, I don't want to shock you, but I have no other way of telling you this. I want you to know that I am alive and well. I am sorry for the loss of your mother and your grief. You certainly have had a rough couple of years. It is very hard to put on paper all of the emotions I feel, but I still love you very much and want to know if you still care for me.

I did a terrible thing. I defected from the Army and went to Italy during the war. If we ever get together, I will tell you the details of why I did this. I am not making excuses for myself. I did the wrong thing. I want to make it right with you, and I hope you will forgive me. I am having a hard time forgiving myself.

Our anniversary is coming up soon, and the years I have been away from you have been a total waste. My life is a waste without you. I think of all of the dreams we had and the very rich deep love we once shared. Do you think it's possible to have this back again? I hope your answer is yes. If not, I'll understand. I truly will understand if you do not want to have anything to do with me. Sometimes, I sicken myself. However, I need to forgive myself. I hope you will forgive me, and I wait anxiously for your reply. After you read this letter, destroy it. Just save my address. No one can know who I am.

I love you,
Joe

I did not hear from Maria right away. Christmas and New Years came and went. I thought maybe she wouldn't answer at all, but each day when I went for my groceries I stopped to see if I had any mail. A month went by, and I was starting to give up hope when a letter came addressed to me. I stuck it in my pocket and opened it when I got home:

Dear Joe,

When I first read your letter, I was so angry with you that I could not answer. All this time you were alive and had me grieving for you like you were dead. Now you want to come back to me and start over. Except for the fact that I never stopped loving you, I would have thrown the letter away and never answered it. Coupled with my anger is a deep abiding love. When I took my vows with you, they were for life. I meant it when I said, "Until death do us part."

I thought you were dead, but I could never get you out of my heart. I was engaged for a short time to your cousin Nicolas, but

I constantly compared him to you and knew it wouldn't work out, so we broke up. Joe, I am very confused and can talk to no one about this. What kind of life would we have? I would have to leave my family and friends and never look back. Could I do that? I don't know. I need more time to think about this; but be assured of one thing--I never stopped loving you.

All my love,
Maria

After receiving Maria's letter, I was hopeful. I thought maybe if she could come up here and we could talk, I could explain everything a little better. So I wrote back:

Dear Maria,
    Please come to see me soon. Come for the weekend. Do not tell anyone where you are going. Take the train to Phoenicia. If you tell me what time the train will be in, I'll meet you at the station. Please come. I know if you do, we can sit down and talk and iron some of these things out.

Love,
Joe

It took about three weeks before I heard from Maria. It was now the third week of February, and she said she would come for the weekend. She would have to come Saturday because she worked on Friday. She would take the 8:00 a.m. train and arrive around noon.

I asked Don for a loan of his car for the weekend. He said I could use the extra one. I was so excited! I worked a half day Saturday and went to the station at noon. It was just a few minutes away, so I knew I would be there on time. I was so excited to meet her that it seemed like an eternity that morning waiting for the train to arrive. At exactly 12 noon, the train pulled up. A couple stepped off the train, then an elderly lady, and then I saw her. My heart skipped and my mouth went dry. I was shaking. How would I look to her? I knew I'd lost some weight, and my hair got a little thinner from nerves. I was trying to contain myself, and I couldn't. Maria was very composed and smiling as she stepped off the train and walked slowly to me. I had to catch my breath. She looked beautiful and not a day older. She hugged me and said, "Joe." I immediately said, "Don't call me that. I have another name. Please call me Danny."

All she said was, "Oh!" I had to keep my emotions under wraps. I hugged her and gave her a kiss on the cheek and told her how happy I was to see her. I escorted her to the car with her small bag and drove to the cottage. It was only a few minutes, and we didn't say much. When we got out of the car, we went inside and I fixed us some sandwiches and soup. It was so good having her near me. I felt like I was dreaming, like it just wasn't true.

After lunch we sat on the studio couch, and I told her the whole story. She was very quiet, trying to understand. She understood most of it; some of it she did not. I told her about the papers I'd taken from the farmer, and how she had to call me by my new name, Danny. I suggested that we take a ride in the car and see the country, and she agreed. We took a long ride through the countryside together. Maria thought the area was beautiful. When we came back, I made some hamburgers for supper and we listened to the radio for awhile. I told her I would sleep on the studio couch, and she could sleep in the bedroom. I did not want to rush her. She did not know what she wanted to do yet, so I thought it best if we took it slow.

The next morning we went to church, came back, and had a big breakfast of bacon, eggs, pancakes, coffee and rolls. The train was leaving at 10 o'clock, so we didn't have too much time left. Maria had said very little the day before, so I prodded her into telling me how she felt. She started by saying, "I don't know, Danny, or whoever you are. You want me to come here and leave my family and friends, live a lie, and not have friends for fear I'll say the wrong thing. That's a lot to ask, and I don't know if I can do that. I'll have to think and pray about it because I don't know if this kind of life would be enough for me or for us. We may end up hating each other. I don't know if I could do this. It's against everything I believe in. I love you, but I don't know if I could live that kind of a life."

I said, "I understand. It's a lot to ask, and I know what it's like. It is a very lonely life. Think about it, and keep in touch, and we'll come to some kind of conclusion." I took Maria to the train and kissed her good-bye. I had no feelings one way or the other about the outcome of all this. I couldn't tell if she was willing to take me back or not.

The next few weeks went by, and we sent some notes back and forth, but I didn't have a distinct feeling about what she would do. I couldn't invite her for Easter because her family would wonder where she was, so I asked her to come the following week. We followed the same routine. I picked her up at the station, and we came back to the cottage, but this time I had a plan.

We had lunch, and after lunch, we sat on the studio couch and I said to her, "Maria, I have beaten myself up. I have downed myself and all but destroyed myself. I can't go on like this anymore. I am torn to pieces. What I would like to do is turn myself in to the authorities. I don't like the thoughts of it, and I know it will be horrible; but if I pay my debt to society, I think I can offer you a better life without lies and deception. We can live anywhere and not have to worry. What do you say?"

Maria threw herself into my arms and cried. She said, "I knew you would figure out a way for us. Yes, Joe, I would be proud of you if you did the right thing and turned your life around. I love you more than life itself. When I heard you might be dead, I wanted to die. I thought I could not go on without you. You were my life, my hope. The only thing that held me together was my faith."

"Maria, will you wait for me for as long as it takes?"

"Yes, Joe", she replied, "I will. I would wait for you forever because you are my life, my love, my whole world. When we were pronounced man and wife, we became one. Remember the forget-me-nots? We are one forever, and this time nothing will come between us."

"I love you, Maria, with all of my heart. I am so glad I didn't die overseas. Otherwise, we would have never had this moment. Well, Mrs. Roman, would you like to retire with me?"

She shook her head, and as we went into the bedroom and closed the door, we were man and wife in every way.

Printed in the United States
33856LVS00002B/37

9 781413 707397